LEAVING
WISHVILLE

Library of Congress Control Number: 2019918355

ISBN 978-1-7341745-0-2 (paperback)

ISBN 978-1-7341745-2-6 (hardcover)

ISBN 978-1-7341745-1-9 (ebook)

This book is a work of fiction. Names, characters, places, and incidents either are the product of the author's imagination or are used fictitiously. Any resemblance to actual events, businesses, companies, locales or persons, living or dead, is entirely coincidental.

Cover design by Cakamura Designs

Interior formatting by Melissa Williams Design

Published by Lost Island Press
San Jose, California
www.lostislandpress.com

www.leavingwishville.com

www.meltorrefranca.com

MEL TORREFRANCA

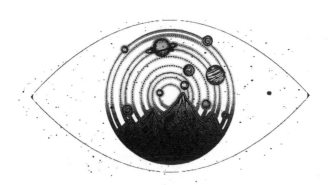

LEAVING
WISHVILLE

LOST ISLAND
PRESS

For my childhood friends,
wherever you are

Part I

nina

CHAPTER 1

goodbye

It would make a tragic story. Benji Marino, fourteen, kills himself on a venture to paradise. A catchy title for the announcements on Wishville News before the morning weather report. On the other hand, he might survive.

Benji emerged around the corner of Wishville Junior High, eyes locked on a hill in the distance. All he had to do was make it to Candy Road and his escape would be a sweet success. He held his breath as he passed the school baseball field.

"Nice one. Back in line." Benji could recognize the man's voice from a mile away. Coach Hendrick was notorious for never using a microphone at school events. After fifteen years of coaching baseball and softball teams he'd reached the conclusion that screaming was the only way to gain respect from middle schoolers.

"Mortimer, you're up next." There was a pause, and his mustache twitched as if going through a seizure. "Mortimer!"

A *clang* came from the fence. Benji refused to look.

"Hey." Chloe Mortimer ran her fingers along the wires, walking at a matched pace. "Where you headed?"

Chloe was the youngest student in his eighth-grade class with a birthday at the end of November, but she didn't act the part. She was more mature than most kids their age, gave the best advice, and could have a serious conversation despite her energetic, fidgety nature. Chloe was the type of friend Benji could trust with anything, and although he hated lying to her, he would if he had to. Especially today.

He watched the ground as they walked, his shoes tapping the concrete in rhythm with her cleats clicking the dirt. She had outgrown her cleats months ago, and although they were originally white, they were now yellowed from use. She held a strange attachment to them, and he wondered how long it would take her to buy new ones.

Benji tucked his hands into his sweatshirt pocket and held his head straight, knowing that looking at her would be too painful. "Thought I'd take a walk."

"Oh yeah?" Chloe paused, scooping a softball from the ground. She ran back to his side and tossed it into the sky. "Come on, I know something's up." She held her arm out, and the ball dropped into her palm. "You're planning something crazy, aren't you?"

"Why would you think—"

"Benji, a seagull could lie better than you."

He made the mistake of facing her. Their eyes met through the wire fence, and he froze.

"I get that you're curious, but we're not gonna let you run off into the wild." Her smile was gone now.

"I mean—come on—you may as well throw your own dead body in a gutter."

Coach Hendrick shouted for Chloe through cupped palms, but she didn't turn away. Benji folded his fingers inside his pocket, waiting for the right moment. When a few girls from the team shouted *Chloe* in unison, she looked over her shoulder, and he ran.

She dropped the softball and shot after him. The gate slammed shut, followed by the hollow steps of her cleats against the sidewalk. It took three weeks of self-preparation for this day, and although Chloe wouldn't let him get away, he wouldn't let her stop him either.

"Listen!" Her breathing staggered, barely allowing the words to escape her lips. "You think no one would care? How would your mom react?" She gasped and sprinted with her last bit of energy, a final attempt to catch him.

He saw the tilted sign of Candy Road ahead, and by the time he reached it, Chloe was far behind, hands on her knees, panting.

With a forced grin, he hiked up the hill.

Chloe had been one of his best friends since first grade, and it was unfortunate that the last memory she'd have of him was the moment he disappeared into the trees. Sweat formed at the creases of his floppy hair. He rubbed the mess out of his face with a tense hand. *It's okay*, he thought. *It'll be worth it.*

Candy Road was close enough to the edge of Wishville that no one dared to breathe its air. Since the bridge was never maintained, neither was the road. Roots of surrounding evergreen trees grew into it, forming cracks for moss to grow and bumps designed to trip. But to

Benji it was better this way. The road was steep, so he used the roots to push his feet forward. Candy Road had grown a set of natural stairs.

When he reached the top, he paused at the base of the bridge in nostalgia. The water gently flowing at the horizon, the sour scent of damp dirt, the gray sky looming over him. He couldn't remember the last time he'd been here, yet the atmosphere was familiar. Comforting.

He took his first step onto the wide platform of concrete and shut his eyes. Living in Wishville his whole life, he had grown deaf to the ocean, but today the waves thrashed beneath him violently. He opened his eyes to reveal a rusty sign across bridge, surrounded by a sea of redwood trees. *LEAVING WISHVILLE*, it read. This marked the end of his journey.

His grip on the straps of his backpack tightened as he peeked over the bridge railing. His school by the shore, the town park a few blocks to the east, everything was there. Further north were the brick buildings of the town square, Main Street running past it. He lifted his head until his nose leveled with a hill on the opposite end of town, of which yielded a single secluded home. Everything he knew, and he was ready to leave it all behind.

"Goodbye, Wishville." Benji waved at the view. Facing the mission before him, he engaged in a staring contest with the sign. After a long blink, a new spark brewed in his eyes.

He took long and speedy strides across the bridge, reaching closer to the end than ever before. The tree branches by the sign reached forward, calling for him to continue. To finally break through Wishville into a new world. His right foot stretched for the border, and the other side of the bridge illuminated with extravagant colors. The vomit green trees, the musty blue sky, the overpowering browns. He could hear the chirping of distant birds suppressing the screaming seagulls that flew over his head. The colors and sounds were so immersing that he couldn't hear the rustling of bushes behind him, the hammering footsteps.

It wasn't until his foot retracted against its will that Benji broke from his daze. He stumbled backwards, the sky fading gray, the trees losing their animation, the dirt as bland and cold as ever. The only colors available were the few familiar wisps of brick-red hair that flashed his vision. "Boo!"

A hand released his backpack with a sturdy throw, and Benji crashed into the railing by the waist. The hungry waves jumped beneath the bridge, trying to reach him. He turned around, head spinning.

To his left was James Koi. He wore a white collared shirt underneath his sweater vest and the latest designer shoes. James had always been a natural at fashion, which was odd since no one could imagine him standing in front of a mirror. Perhaps his elegant style was simply an accident every morning. He completed the outfit with an expressionless mask, not a single fold on his forehead or a tilt of his lips either up or down. "You're going to get yourself killed."

To Benji's right was Samantha Perkins, who went exclusively by Sam. Benji almost smiled at the sight of her wearing last year's school jogathon shirt, which she didn't participate in. She tucked her hands into the pockets of her fluffy jacket, and a few chuckles escaped her lips. "You should've seen the look on your face." She paused her laughter to imitate the exact moment. "Boo!" Leaning over, she broke into hysteria until her cheeks were as red as her knotted hair.

Benji could never understand her. Sometimes everything was funny and other times everything was somehow meant to insult her. Sam's emotions were as predictable as flipping a coin.

When Sam extinguished her humor, James repositioned himself next to Benji. "It's illogical to leave." He gave Benji's head a shove from above, taking advantage of his height. "You're smarter than this."

The idea of staying in Wishville sickened him. "I know it doesn't make sense." He pointed to the end of the bridge. "But don't you guys ever wonder what's out there?"

"Couldn't care less." Sam crossed her arms, and her raspy voice smoothened. "Although I guess it's different when your dad goes missing."

James glared at her, and she pursed her lips with raised brows.

Benji spun around and set his arms on the bridge railing. "There's a lot I wish I knew." He watched the seagulls zoom across the horizon. Left and right. Up and down. Wherever they wanted to.

"By the way, we were Plan B." Sam chuckled. "I can't believe Chloe couldn't talk you out of it. You're such a pain."

Benji shot for the end of the bridge, but James formed a wall in front of him.

Sam stepped away, and a twig snapped beneath her sneaker. "Let's go back."

Knowing James wouldn't move, Benji tucked his frozen hands into the pockets of his sweatshirt and walked back the way he came. As he took his first step down Candy Road, he peeked over his shoulder to spot the *LEAVING WISHVILLE* sign one last time. He held his head low, the glow in his eyes gone.

"You know, we're only doing this because we care," Sam said.

He scanned the ground for the next root to step on. "How did you know?"

She looked to James, asking permission to tell. He nodded.

"Well you were acting all suspicious. Took *way* more notes during class than usual."

"You searched my binder, didn't you?"

"You weren't taking notes on prepositional phrases, that's the thing." Sam's sneaker chipped against a root, but she caught her balance and recovered. "You literally wrote your entire escape plan. Date, time, *everything*."

James ran a hand through his hair. "Not smart."

"Well," Benji said. "I guess I'll have to be smarter next time." He smiled, and Sam jabbed him in the side.

"Are you sure you wouldn't like to stay for dinner?" Mr. Koi asked.

"I've got a violin lesson, and my dad has another meeting tonight." Sam zipped her jacket with a stiff arm. "I can't."

Mr. Koi nodded as she turned away. "Next time,"

he said, but they all knew it wouldn't happen. Sam was one of the busiest kids in school, always attending fancy dinners, meetings, important events. She despised her tight schedule, yet Benji considered it a bargain for a family like hers.

Mr. Koi waited until Sam was out of sight before shutting the door. That's when the investigation began. He straightened his tie and glanced between them. "You three were out late today."

Benji was too focused on the room to notice him. The Koi household was located on Main Street, which ran along the town square. The houses on Main ranged from all different sizes, each designed with its own unique architecture. James's home was one of the larger ones. His parents owned and managed Sequoia Bank and the town's department store, Wishville Depot. Benji knew such a wealthy family deserved a fitting home, but he couldn't keep the jealousy from pouring in. Every time he'd come home with James he'd always stop to admire the raised ceilings, floors of soft wood, and sunlight showering from windows that were only covered at dark.

"Rebecca phoned me. She's been worried sick." Mr. Koi added. This time, Benji heard him.

"Sorry."

The man smiled, and his teeth glimmered in the light. "I'll let her know you've made it back." Before Mr. Koi could proceed to the rest of his questioning, the two boys hid upstairs to get some peace before the meal.

Benji appreciated James's room simply because it was the opposite of his. There wasn't one speck of dust, and everything was placed elegantly where it belonged.

Shelves along the wall were trickled with strange puzzles, all of which Benji gave up on solving years ago. Even the wooden trinkets James called *beginner level* were enough to braid his mind into twists.

Then there were the books. Those were the main attraction of James's room. Benji tried placing his head in a position where he couldn't see a book and found that the only place possible was the ceiling. He respected his friend's love for literature, as much as a non-reader possibly could.

"Hey." Benji sat on James's bed and watched his feet dangle over the floor. If only he had been a few inches taller. "Sorry about—you know—trying to leave town and all."

James opened his favorite book, *Sharpner's Peak*. He read it so often that if someone were to spout a random page number, he could recite the first paragraph from memory. He leaned back in his desk chair and brought the pages closer to his eyes, his lips glued together.

"I guess part of me wants to know what happened to my dad." Benji folded his fingers together, watching them turn red. "And the other half is just dreading the spring festival."

"Shh . . ." James looked up from the pages and smiled. "You've wasted enough of my reading time already." That was his way of saying, "*I forgive you.*"

Benji's fingers relaxed. He hauled his backpack off the floor and slipped out his sketchbook and a charcoal pencil. Of all things to pack for his escape, he chose to bring his drawings. A stupid choice, considering he didn't know what might be out there. A knife, spare clothes, or a peanut butter and jelly sandwich would have been a smarter move. But when Benji had stood in the center of his room, searching for something that mattered, his sketchbook was all that caught his eye.

It was a silent moment. Benji appreciated that about his friendship with James. They didn't need to talk all the time. His friendship wasn't like Sam's, where he'd have to constantly tune out her complaining, or Chloe, where they spoke a lot about nothing. James and he would often sit in silence. Reading, drawing. Flipping, erasing. Silence was all they had in common, and that was enough.

Benji continued a drawing from last week. A stretch of land without trees, sprinkled with buildings resembling diamonds more than homes. Something about drawing landscapes and strange buildings had always caught his attention.

Mr. Koi knocked on the door half an hour later before peeking his head inside. "You should get seated," he said. "I'll wake Nina."

The two nodded, sliding downstairs and into the dining room. Although Benji had stuffed his sketchbook into his backpack, James didn't have the strength to leave his book upstairs. While he sat at the table reading, Benji watched the steam billow from the serving plates. The fresh broccoli coupled with the sour aroma of lemony shrimp made his mouth water. On the far end of the table was a giant bowl from Chowdies. That was the best place in town to buy clam chowder. It was also the only place.

"Mom's not here?" James spoke behind the pages. Even without a book Benji hadn't noticed Mr. Koi enter the room. Some would argue the Kois' intuition was strong enough to call a superpower.

"Visiting some friends." Mr. Koi sat and scooped a generous helping of shrimp onto his plate. He paused and gave his son a stern look in the eye. "Put the book down."

James frowned and stuck a penny between the pages to hold his place.

Nina hovered into the room after her father. She sat, flung her thick, chocolate braids behind her shoulders, and waited for Mr. Koi to serve her. She blinked slowly, and Benji could tell by the way she stared into space that she had been sleeping all day. She took a lot of naps for an eleven-year-old. She took a bite of broccoli, coughing as she choked it down.

Mr. Koi set his hand on the table. "Don't force yourself."

Nina glanced at Benji for a moment, then nodded at her plate.

Although Nina and James were only two years apart, they may as well have been six. For starters, James was tall for his age, and his doctor expected him to exceed six feet and surpass his father. Nina, on the other hand, hardly looked older than eight. She had a strange gravitation to dresses, even though most kids her age made the quick transition to jeans and plaid shirts. Benji wasn't sure if Nina was short because she was sick, or if it had to do with genetics. It seemed the one thing they did have in common, however, was their perfect skin. Their tone was stuck somewhere between Mr. Koi's smooth cocoa skin, and Mrs. Koi's pale tan. A creamy butterscotch tone, complimented with their honey brown eyes. Every time Benji noticed their skin he was instantly ashamed of his freckles. He tilted his head downward, hoping they might be less prominent that way.

"It's been awhile since you've joined us for dinner," Mr. Koi straightened the collar of his shirt. "How are you?"

"I'm doing great, actually." Benji smiled, keeping his head low.

"And your mother? Everything going well with her?"

"You know," Benji said, "everything's always the same."

"Good." Mr. Koi pushed his glasses further up the bridge of his nose. "That's good."

A silence fell over the table. Benji was plating his food when Mr. Koi continued his investigation. "I hate to pry," he said, shoveling a spoonful of chowder into his mouth, "but what were you three doing today?"

Benji's hands fumbled, and the serving spoon splattered on the table, spilling broccoli across the wood. "Sorry." He grimaced and transferred the pieces to his plate one at a time.

James cleared his throat. "Sam suggested we see the ocean."

Mr. Koi nodded, although they both knew he wasn't convinced. Out of all the parents in Wishville, most considered him the least easygoing. Like James and Nina, Mr. Koi was an expert at puzzles, but not the wooden kind in particular. He set down his spoon, humored eyes staring through his rectangular glasses. "You all must really like waves."

James stopped chewing, stuck in thought.

Benji was always mesmerized by the Kois' conversations. The family wasn't known for talking much, but they always got their point across. It was almost a competition for who could talk the least.

While James picked his words carefully, Benji's brain went into a state of panic. He couldn't keep his mouth shut. "We were—you know—" Benji gulped. "Counting the seagulls."

"*Counting the seagulls*," Mr. Koi repeated. He chuckled and took another bite. "And how many did you count?"

James's answer was instantaneous.

"One-hundred-and-seventeen." He shot Benji a disappointed look.

"How did you make sure you didn't count one twice?"

Mr. Koi was nothing more than a rock on a smooth path, waiting for James to trip as he ran. The pattern would continue until either James messed up, or Mr. Koi gave in and nodded at his persuasive son with pride. Benji switched focus between the two as questions were spouted and logically answered. He folded his fingers in anticipation of who would win the game.

That's when Nina pushed her plate of food in front of her and gulped a monstrous sip of water, forcing another bite. She stared at Benji deep in the eyes, and at that moment they were two pits of black fire. He found himself lost in them, and his hands began to shake.

"Benji," Mr. Koi said. "Is something wrong?"

"Oh—uh, no." He peeled his eyes from Nina and prepared another bite with his spoon. "I'm fine."

"What did you do today?" It was Nina asking the question this time.

Benji hesitated, not sure why she'd ask. When he opened his mouth to spout the same lie they repeated throughout the meal, the words clotted in his throat. "I—well—"

"What did you do today?" she repeated. Her tone of voice reminded Benji of a teacher during a verbal quiz, testing with the answer in mind.

Benji's hands went stiff. "Like I said, we were counting seagulls." He tried to sound as natural as possible, but his voice was a tad higher than normal, and he could tell by the way her fingers tightened around her fork that she wasn't convinced.

"I'm not hungry." She slammed her fork onto her plate and stood so fast that the chair legs squealed against the bamboo floor.

"Are you okay?" Mr. Koi was by her side immediately. "Feeling dizzy?"

Nina looked back at Benji. Something in her eyes was different this time, but he couldn't figure out what it was.

"Yeah," she said. "I'm feeling *sick*."

CHAPTER 2

blueberry

They called the place *Blueberry*.

It was an ostracized building in the forest. Not so far from civilization that it was difficult to access, but far enough that most people curious to see it avoided the trouble. Hiding in plain sight, the rotting shed reserved itself for those capable of recognizing its value. And so it became a safe place for the four kids. Their second home. A jar of sparkling memories.

Chloe collapsed onto the tattered rug in the center of the room. "I can't believe it's been six years since we found this place." She flopped onto her back, and her hazelnut hair spread around her like a lion's mane. "Life wouldn't be worth living without Blueberry."

Benji shut the door behind him and leaned against it. What started as a childish game of hide-and-seek resulted in one of his favorite places in Wishville. He had found it tucked within a circle of thick redwood trees, moss crusted over the open door and layering the deck in a fuzzy green tarpaulin. It wasn't until a few years later that they heard it was some dead lady's storage shed for her moss gardening equipment, which explained the unnatural growth. They had already thought so dearly of Blueberry that they didn't let such a fact intimidate them, so instead they convinced themselves it was hilarious.

"Think we should rename it?" Benji observed the second door on the other side of the room, the wood all cracked and splintery. The molding was covered in literal mold, some dark specks that he would rather not consider the safety of, and the floor had gaps so big between the boards that it seemed the only place safe enough to avoid an amputation was the rug. "More like *Rotting Blueberry*."

Chloe shot up, pointing a firm finger at the ceiling. "He didn't mean that!"

Benji joined her on the floor with a chuckle. Chloe had brought the rug to Blueberry a few years ago from her attic, where her older sister hid a lot of her parents' old things.

"We can't rename Blueberry. She doesn't deserve that. Come on, you're practically the founder." After untangling both of her shoelaces, she tied them again in perfect bows. Chloe had always found strange ways to occupy her short attention span. "And it's all because you wanted to play in the forest, of all places. I remember searching for you guys and out of nowhere, I hear you screaming my name from inside of some random shack."

"Yeah, and you were scared to death." He ran his hands along the softened wool until his fingers met the frills along the edges. Although old, the carpet's red and gold designs were vibrant, its geometrical shapes and twists mesmerizing.

"Well you can't blame me. It looks like the kind of place you go to get stabbed and ground into patties."

For a moment Benji forgot that the shed lacked windows. He observed the two wooden entrances, and when he finally remembered, went back to playing with the rug. "Sam said five, didn't she?"

"Oh, she's coming. Might be late, though. Heard her family was meeting with the Zhaos tonight." She raised her head from the floor with a mischievous grin. "Speaking of the Zhaos . . ."

"No."

"Why?"

Benji's face went hot. "I can't."

"Ah, so you're brave enough to leave town, but too scared to tell a girl how you feel?" Chloe reached to untie her shoelace again, but kicked her foot away to stop herself. "At least give Audrey a letter or something."

"You kidding me?" Benji rubbed his forehead, feeling dizzy. "That's even worse! Not in a million years."

"Aw," Chloe said, pinching her cheeks, "the Benji is blushing."

"Plus," Benji said softly, "she likes James."

The room fell silent. Her eyes lingered on him for a while, but he didn't dare look. The floorboards squealed below them, and the ceiling crackled like a fire.

"Hey." Her voice was softer this time. "I think we should talk about yesterday."

Benji didn't look at her.

"I know how you feel. It was hard enough that my mom died giving birth to me. Then my dad got sick. It felt like the end of the world." A strand of hair fell from her bun, and she tucked it behind her ear. "My dad used to say that when something bad happens, you either keep living, you live dead, or you die. I chose to live, but if you disappeared too, what would I do then?"

"Oh, I don't know." He smiled at the floor. "Maybe you wouldn't have to run out of your softball practices anymore."

"Really?" She reached for that same strand of hair and twisted it between her fingers. "You're more important than my stupid softball practices."

Sam stormed in. She was wearing a dress for the first time since Wishville Elementary's third-grade picnic. The fabric was a faded red, and her hair nearly blended right into it. She huffed away their stares and leaned against the wall. "Don't ask."

"We didn't," Benji said.

She kicked off her dirty sneakers and explained anyway. "My dad had a meeting with the Zhao family about job opportunities or something. My brothers didn't have to go, but guess who did?" Her eyes narrowed until Benji could no longer see them. "My mom wanted me to *keep Audrey entertained.*"

Chloe took down her bun, bored of messing with one strand. "Complaining about Audrey again?"

"My dad asked her if she could play a song for us on the violin. And guess what? She plays the *exact* song I've been working on." Sam felt the callouses on her left fingers. "Something about her is just—it's off."

Benji couldn't stop himself from smiling. If there was nothing for Sam to complain about she'd always create something. Complaining was her favorite hobby. And for some reason, her favorite person to complain about was Audrey Zhao, the most perfect girl in school. No, in town. The most perfect girl in Wishville.

"Well," Chloe said, "your dress is nice."

Sam pushed herself off the wall and sat next to Chloe. "Stop."

"Oh, come on." She leaned into her shoulder playfully. "The dinner couldn't have been *that* bad."

Benji sighed. Sam probably liked Chloe more than anyone simply because she fed her flames of complaints. A lifetime as friends and Chloe still hadn't learned to ignore them. James would say it was ignorant, but Benji assumed it was a girl thing. The love for complaints.

"It was awful." Sam licked her lips and cringed. "Audrey's family literally only eats fish. You know how much I *hate* fish."

James still hadn't shown. After a few glances at the door, Sam shrugged and slipped over to the crooked cabinets, scavenging for some snacks she had set aside. She found a bag of potato chips, unraveled it, and plopped it in the center of the carpet for them to share. Chloe snatched one. It was stale.

"Gross."

"Would you rather have *no* potato chips?" Sam asked.

"Yes." Chloe nodded her head as she slipped the chip back into the bag. "Definitely. Yes."

"Don't put it back in!" Sam yanked the bag from her and passed it to Benji.

He laughed, his hair hopping on his head. "I think I'll pass."

Chloe reached to put her hair back into a ponytail, tired of playing with it. They were all acting normal, ignoring the fact that James was still missing. But unlike them, Benji had a limit for how long he could contain his curiosity.

"Does anyone know where James is?"

He hadn't been acting strange throughout the day. Only read books in class and started worksheets before their teachers finished instructions. The usual James. But this was the first time he had ever been late to a meeting at Blueberry.

Sam stuffed a few chips down her throat. "He probably forgot."

"Suspicious." Chloe squinted. "Very suspicious."

But James never forgets. He hadn't forgotten anything since the day he left his essay on his desk at home, distracted by a new book. It was a rainy day. He had walked out in the middle of class, fetched his essay, and came back dripping wet with the ruined papers in hand. Not one emotion crossed his face, but Benji could tell the boy had never undergone such shame.

"We still need to figure out how to punish you for trying to leave us." Chloe hummed to herself. "How about five dollars apiece?"

Sam elbowed her in the side. "That's way too little!"

"Whoa there." Benji raised a hand. "How about nothing?"

"Twenty bucks or I tell your mom." Sam crossed her arms and raised her chin, staring him down.

Benji's soul slipped. The image of adults discovering his attempted escape left him petrified. One word about him trying to leave and the whole town would be in a frenzy, but he pushed the fear aside. Sam might not have been the quietest person at school, but they'd been close friends for as long as he could remember.

"Don't you find it fishy that no one ever comes here?"

They stared, waiting for more.

"That book we're reading in class. *The Mysticals.* Each chapter someone new moves into town, and the kids meet them and learn about where they're from." He frowned. "I asked Mr. Trenton why we never have strangers move to Wishville. And he responded by saying, 'Benji, *The Mysticals* is fiction.'"

"I remember that," Chloe said.

"But it wasn't just *The Mysticals.*" He shook his head. "It's happened in so many books we've been forced to read. There'd be a new neighbor next door. Or someone would move to the other side of the world. People came and went from all over the place and it . . . I don't know. It doesn't make sense."

"Don't be an idiot." Sam laughed into her hand, shaking her head. "There's lots of books with supernatural stuff in them, too. Doesn't mean *that's* real."

Their meeting at Blueberry lasted longer than expected, and he had spent the majority of his walk home under a blanket of stars. Expecting a lecture, he took his time opening the door.

But there was no lecture. Only a girl.

Nina stood in the dining room, her creamy eyes bloodshot and dry. Mr. Koi wrapped an arm around her. She observed her shoes and pulled tenderly at her braids.

James was the only one seated. He sat at the opposite head of the table, as far away from everyone as possible. His world of isolation broke for a moment as Benji caught his attention. He waved without a smile, pulled the pages closer to his face, and disappeared. Rebecca, on the other hand, was fully engaged. Her forehead was smeared in wrinkles, her lips pursed. She wanted to speak, but something was holding her back.

"Go on." Mr Koi's grip tightened on Nina's shoulder. "Tell him." His voice was sharp, cloaked in a layer of butter, neither sweet nor bitter.

The realization hit Benji in a storm. The way Nina had questioned him last night was suspicious. He wasn't sure how, but she knew. She knew all about his plan to leave town, and she told the adults everything. All of it. His secret was loose. It was over.

But when Nina spoke, Benji's arms relaxed.

"I'm sorry." She clung to the fabric of her black dress as she raised her chin. Inside her eyes was an ocean of raging darkness.

Nina's nervousness made him uneasy. She had always been like the rest of the Kois, dictator of her emotions, reserving energy for chosen recreation rather than pointless worries. Yet there was something about her facial expression today—something about the way her lips drooped and her skin lightened a shade—that made Benji think she was about to cry.

Mr. Koi must have sensed it too. He pulled her closer to his side, and she grabbed her wrist tightly, the color in her fingers fading.

The dining room, usually filled with a thick layer of gray air, now had a menacing red film. As much as Benji wanted to believe it was real, he knew it was all in his mind. The curiosity seeped through his sight. Red. A color of interesting change.

There was an odd hue to her eyes now. A dash of rose in a freshly burned forest.

"Sorry about what?"

She hadn't done anything to hurt him. Their past interactions were nothing more than a quick nod of the head when passing each other in the Koi house, and maybe the occasional exchange of words at dinner. Nina had always been a recluse, confined to her room to sleep or read aloud to the wall. Even Sam and Chloe hardly spoke to her. Nina was never shy around them. She was simply disinterested, and as a result, they returned the disinterest, acknowledging her not as Nina, a clever eleven-year-old genius, but as James's little sister. The sick one.

Nina's fingers loosened on her wrist until she let go, her hands dangling by her sides. "I don't feel well."

Mr. Koi's pushed Nina away, resting a gentle palm on her forehead. He raised his chin in Rebecca's direction. "Fever."

"What can I do?" Rebecca asked.

"Don't worry yourself." Mr. Koi was already guiding Nina to the door. He turned to James, his voice hardening. "Put the book away."

Then the Kois left. It was only Benji and Rebecca now, as it always was. Rebecca made her rounds through the house, shutting off the bright lights. The red tint vanished, replaced by the usual gray fog of normality. "Did something happen between you two? You can tell me the truth."

"I don't know anything about Nina," he said, and that was all it took for Rebecca to believe him. She poured herself a glass of water. "Why were you home so late again?"

There it was, the lecture he was waiting for.

"I was with Sam and Chloe."

She wrapped her hands around the cold glass. "You need to tell me these things ahead of time. How do I know if something happened to you?" She took a sip of water. "I want you heading straight home as soon as that bell rings, alright?"

"You know, I could get home faster if I had a bike."

"You could get hurt."

"Everyone at school has one except me."

"You don't get it, Benji." Rebecca smiled gently. "What do you wanna eat? Are you cold? I'll make some—"

"I'll have cereal."

"The sugar content is—"

"Look, the festival's tomorrow." Benji stood on his toes and selected his favorite bowl from the cabinet. "If you're gonna make me go, just give me a break tonight." He was about to slam it onto the countertop, but stopped himself. His fingers loosening, he set the bowl delicately onto the granite.

"You should be proud to go. It's in honor of Scott this year."

"Yeah, another reminder that he's gone." Benji retrieved a box of chocolate flakes from the cabinet. "Sounds fun."

"That's not what it's—"

"You know you can say it." Benji faced her. "Hiding pictures in the back cabinet doesn't magically make me think he never existed."

"I want what's best for you."

"And that's why I could never join the soccer team? Because you want what's best for me?"

"Soccer is dangerous. You could get hurt."

"No, Mom. I know he loved soccer." The picture flashed through his mind. His father standing in front of Wishville Elementary's field with a goofy grin and a soccer ball under his arm. He saw it a million times. Not when Rebecca was home, of course. It was in a chipped frame, tossed in a cabinet beneath their living room radio.

"Benji, you're all I have left of him."

"Well I'm not Dad!" He grabbed the cereal box, pausing as his fingers wrapped around the edge. "I'm just . . . me."

Rebecca sipped her water, watching him through the bottom of the glass. She gulped and set the cup on the counter. "I think we both need some rest. It's been a long day." She gave Benji a soft tap on the shoulder before entering the hall. "You'll have fun tomorrow. Promise."

Benji shut his eyes, hoping to cleanse the stress from his mind. He'd deal with the festival tomorrow, but for now, all that mattered was the bowl of cereal. Chocolate flakes had been his favorite for as long as he could remember. When Rebecca allowed him to eat these *empty calories*, he always made it count. There was a specific way he prepared it. A recipe he'd been perfecting for years.

First, the flakes. He'd fill them nearly to the brim, then seep the milk halfway. The milk was the secret. Too little and the flakes were too dry. Too much and it become soggy too fast.

After his perfect bowl was poured, he stuck a spoon inside and headed to his room, shutting off the last kitchen light.

As Benji sat at his desk that night, eating his dinner, he couldn't help but think of Nina.

He set his spoon in the bowl and leaned back, gazing at the ceiling. "Sorry for what?"

Eventually, the question vanished from Benji's mind, and he resumed his meal in silence.

CHAPTER 3

festival

About a month ago, Mayor Perkins had knocked on their door, requesting to speak with Rebecca. He wore a charming smile as he entered their home, announcing that this year's end-of-spring festival would be dedicated to Scott Marino. Each year it was dedicated to someone new, usually a person who contributed to the town. Last year's was for a man named Greg Shirley, whom most people had never heard of, but apparently led the project of building the town square generations ago.

"If it weren't for Scott's ten-day experiment, we wouldn't know the truth about how dangerous it is to leave," the mayor said.

Hearing about this special dedication had only encouraged Benji to follow through with his plan. He had decided to leave town before the festival, on May 4th, but now it was May 6th, and he was still here. He had grown so used to the idea of being gone by the festival that the thought of attending after his failed escape made him nauseous. He did everything to resist. Faked being sick. Claimed he had homework. Pretended he was too exhausted in the morning in hopes that Rebecca would let him sleep in. Unfortunately, Benji had no skills in lying, and Rebecca dragged him into the crowded town square without hesitation.

It was the heart of Wishville. A giant block of concrete with a fountain in the middle and a wooden platform at the end, all backed by a wall of redwood trees protecting them from the icy ocean. The entirety of the courtyard was sandwiched between two rows of brick buildings. Clumps of restaurants, book stores, and tiny boutiques. They were spaced only a couple of feet apart, making the area interesting for a game of tag. As long as one could fit between building without getting stuck.

Seaside Cafe was busier than usual. Many had decided to get a hot cup of coffee before the festival began. Next to the cafe was Ms. Camille's flower shop, deserted, with a *closed* sign hung on the window. She would never choose work over such a special occasion. And across from the cafe was Chowdies. Slightly less populated, but perhaps some people were more in the mood for Wishville's famous clam chowder than a warm drink.

Musicians stood on the raised platform in the courtyard, legs spread wide and chins held high. The employees at Chowdies filled the room, excited for their double payday. Attending the festival wasn't mandatory, but everyone went by choice. That is, everyone except the man on Eudora Hill. Oliver Stricket, they called him. His lack of presence went largely unnoticed, perhaps even appreciated by the few who thought of him.

This year's festival was the same as Benji had always remembered it. Parents raided the discounted shops.

Kids played tag, zipping between brick buildings and hiding behind strangers' backs. One boy even managed to get onto the roof of Chowdies, which was a mystery for everyone. "We love the festival!" he shouted into the air, and his friends at the bottom giggled until their parents came to the scene and ordered him down immediately.

The musicians were playing some kind of ugly noise undeserving of being called a song. The lead singer hollered weird notes into the microphone, while the others strummed guitars or banged on the drums in a failed attempt at syncopation. Benji covered his ears. "We really have to be here?" The only thing he liked about the town festival was that the smell of hot dogs overpowered the stench of clams and salty wind.

Rebecca waved at everyone as they passed by. Even complimented one lady's dress. Benji tried to slip away, but she grabbed his arm. "Stay close, okay? Stick with Sam and Chloe, but don't let them drag you anywhere. And if the mayor talks to you, don't say anything reckless. The last thing you want is—"

"Yeah Mom, I got it." He ripped himself from her grip. "Where's James?"

"The Kois aren't coming this year."

"What?" Benji stopped. "Why not?"

"Nina hasn't been feeling well lately. She was transferred to the hospital this morning."

"Hospital? It's that serious?"

Rebecca spotted a friendly face in the crowd and finally left Benji on his own.

He assumed Sam was probably off with Chloe somewhere, so he headed to the edge of the square, avoiding as many people as possible. Instead, he found Chloe. She was wearing a dress with a fuzzy jacket and had a mitt in her left hand. Across from her was their classmate, Jett Griffin, the last person Benji wanted to see at the festival. He was wearing his baseball uniform, most likely as a way to show off, except his cleats were subbed with sandals. A strange look for a strange kid.

"Benji! Sam was looking for you earlier." Chloe raised her hand, and the ball went straight into it.

"Damn, you're not too shabby, Mortimer." Jett crossed his arms with a crooked smirk.

Benji tuned him out. "Where is she?"

"No clue, but if I had to guess, probably as far away from Audrey as possible." Chloe chuckled. "Where's James?"

He looked away. "He's not coming."

Jett shouted through cupped hands. "You gonna throw in the next few years?"

Chloe peeled her arm back, preparing to throw, but her focus was still glued to Benji. "Why not?"

"Nina's in the hospital."

Chloe threw the ball. In only a blink, Benji flinched from the shattering of glass and pottery against the concrete walkway. "The hospital? It's that serious?" She saw the broken window and froze.

Jett lowered his empty mitt from the air, realizing he had missed the ball. He peeked through the gash in Ms. Camille's flower shop and saw it lying on the floor, surrounded by dirt and toppled orchids. He ran a hand through his raven black hair and muttered a few words under his breath.

Benji paused at Chloe's side, watching the scene. He

had to work his hardest to keep from laughing at Jett's frustration. He knew he should probably be concerned over the incident, but he couldn't help it. Jett was always the cause of broken windows. A couple of years ago he had swung a baseball bat so hard it flew out of his hand and shattered the hallway window at school. The next day he was sweeping the classroom as punishment when he *accidentally* waved the metal dustpan right into the sky. And that was only the beginning of his career.

Benji leaned over Chloe's shoulder and lowered his voice. "Why were you passing with Jett?"

"Come on, he's really not a bad guy." Her eyes traced the damage, and the crowd's murmurs increased as news of the broken window spread. "It was my fault, not his. I was shocked, and my throw paid for it. Just kill me now and end my suffering."

As much as Benji had tried to convince Chloe that Jett was an awful person, she never believed him. Of course she didn't. Jett had a soft spot for everyone on the baseball and softball teams. What seemed like a threat to Benji could be perceived as a silly joke to Chloe.

It was only a matter of time before Ms. Camille came running through the square. Her curly white hair bounced around her hips, her heels clicking with obnoxious snaps. When her eyes met the flower shop, there wasn't a dash of surprise in them. She crossed her arms and stared at Jett, waiting for an explanation.

"It wasn't me this time." He held his hands in the air. "I swear, it was Marino over there."

Ms. Camille looked at Benji, and at that point, he couldn't hold it back anymore. He burst into laughter, and had to take a few steps away. It was normal for

Ms. Camille to wear more makeup than even the youthful women in town, but today it was especially heavy. She always took measures to act younger than her age, spreading rumors over which men in town were buying flowers, theorizing all kinds of complex love stories to fill the void of her unmarried soul. Benji wasn't sure what was more comical—the fact that she considered he might be capable of throwing a baseball into her window, or that a bit of lipstick was smeared on her teeth.

"Sorry." Chloe combed her hair with her fingers. "It was me."

Ms. Camille studied her three suspects, weighing the evidence. "I don't care which one of you threw it. Be lucky the festival put me in a good mood." She reached into her purse and tossed Jett a ring of keys. "There's a dustpan in the back closet. Sweep this up, will you?" She slipped back into the crowd, leaving Jett with a red face.

"What are you laughing at, Marino?"

Benji managed to suppress most of his hysteria. "Don't you have some glass to sweep?"

"She should've given the keys to you. I'm not the one who distracted Chloe."

"And I'm not the one who missed the ball."

Jett stepped toward him, yanking his mitt off his hand. "You've sure got a big mouth for the height of a fifth grader."

"Do you guys really have to argue?" Chloe tossed Jett his second mitt, stopping him in his tracks. "It was my fault, okay? Let it go."

She wasn't taking either of their sides, and for Jett, that was win. He shot Benji a crooked smile.

"Greetings!" Mayor Perkin's booming voice blasted through the square.

"Look." Chloe hopped a few times, pointing to the stage. "He's starting his speech." She flew into the busy crowd and disappeared. Soon everyone from school was licking ice cream and crowding below the mayor's stage. Adults came next. Nearly two thousand people crammed into the courtyard, fighting for a decent spot in the crowd. While Jett struggled opening the door to the flower shop, Benji avoided the rush. He planted himself along the outskirts of the crowd, peeking through gaps between towering adults.

"Today is a special day because it marks the ten-year anniversary of Wishville's safety." The crowd cheered, and Benji grew smaller. "One decade ago this town made a group decision to stay safe together, united. Since then we have not lost a soul to the border."

More cheering. Benji watched the glowing faces in disgust.

"Exactly ten years and ten days ago, I lost my best friend to that very border." His voice sent chills through Benji's arms. Everyone listened carefully, and the silence among the masses was perhaps the most frightening part. "Wishville is a family. We stick together. We protect each other." He smiled and made eye contact with as many people as possible. "Because a decade has passed, we are dedicating this year's festival to Scott Marino. He will forever be remembered as the last to leave. Without him, Wishville might have never changed. Without him, our town would not be united."

Benji's stomach churned.

"This will be a great year." The mayor gestured to the

crowd. "My daughter, Samantha, is now in the eighth grade. We also have an amazing high school graduating class who will grow to do great things for Wishville. My three sons look up to them, and it will only be a matter of time before they too stand on that stage."

Benji couldn't take any more of it. He slipped out of the crowd and left the square.

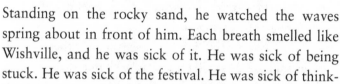

Standing on the rocky sand, he watched the waves spring about in front of him. Each breath smelled like Wishville, and he was sick of it. He was sick of being stuck. He was sick of the festival. He was sick of thinking about his father. He tossed himself onto the sand and groaned at the sky. *I'm sick of gray.* A seagull zipped above him. *I'm sick of seagulls.*

Sam loomed over him before tossing a can onto his stomach. "What's with the gloom?"

Benji flinched from the impact of the can. The condensation dripped over his lap as he sat, proving it was pulled right out of a cooler. "Why are *you* here?"

Sam sat next to him. "I wanna hear his speech as much as you do." Her hair bubbled in the wind, frizzy as always. He could tell by her face that she was equally frustrated. "He thinks he's so great, and everyone believes it."

It was another one of her rants about Mayor Perkins being her father. If anything, she should consider it a privilege. He was the most likable man in town.

Not wanting to make her frustration any worse by

commenting, Benji wiped his hands on his sweater and opened the soda. "Thanks." He took a tiny sip before his reflexes yanked it away from him. *Cherry*. He winced. She knew he hated that flavor.

"Aw, leave me alone. It's all they had." She leaned back, propping herself up by extending her arms behind her. They smelled the salt in the air, the soft support of sand beneath them. A seagull landed, pecking at a package of peanuts that the wind had blown to the shore. "You haven't been thinking about leaving again, have you?"

"I always am." He watched the seagull carefully. It pecked until there were no more specks of peanuts on the sand, flapped its wings, and kicked off the ground into the sky. Benji could only see a hovering speck before he lost sight of it. "Can I ask you something?"

Sam opened her own soda, also cherry. "You can try."

"Is James okay?" Benji drew shapes in the sand with his fingers. "Nina was taken to the hospital this morning. Sounds like she'll be there awhile, but he hasn't even mentioned her lately."

"So *that's* why he wasn't at Blueberry." She frowned. "What's with the weird face?"

"Well . . . something weird happened last night."

She sipped her soda. "Are you gonna tell me or what?"

"When I got home from Blueberry last night, James and Nina were there. She kept apologizing to me, and I have no idea why."

"The Koi's are weird. I gave up trying to understand them years ago." She tapped her fingers against the can in sync with the latest song she'd been practicing. "She's probably being overdramatic about something stupid."

The two sat in silence for a while, an unnatural occurrence for Sam. They sipped their sodas and winced at the taste of artificial cherry. Benji could hear the musicians starting their ugly music back at the square, marking the end of the mayor's speech. He was trying to decipher the lyrics when Sam spoke again. "You wanna talk about it?"

"About what?"

"Your dad." Another sip. "Leaving Wishville. All that."

Benji stood, kicked off his shoes, and removed his socks.

"Benji, it's dangerous."

Ignoring her, he ran to the shore and traced his toes along the freezing waterline. The damp sand and wind brushing against his face sent goosebumps to his arms. He took another step.

Sam had caught up to him by now. "You're such an idiot." Her shoes were still on.

"Oh, have some fun." He rolled his jeans and let the water run to his calves.

"Alright, that's enough." Sam rushed toward him as the waves receded, backing away when they came back stronger. "Seriously, Benji. It's not like humans can swim."

"And how do you know that?"

"Invisibility, swimming, telepathy. You know, things called *superpowers*." She crossed her arms. "We don't live in a fairy tale. If the current takes you, there's no coming back."

"And what do you think is out there?" He pointed to the horizon. "What's past that weird line in the sky?"

"I used to wonder that too." Sam took another step away. "Listen, my dad says a lot of stupid stuff, but there's one thing he's right about."

Benji turned around to face her, feet still submersed.

"Whatever's past that bridge is dangerous. Any idiot could figure that out. How come everyone who left never came back? Your dad left to answer that question, promising to return in ten days. And still, poof! Ten years later, and he's still gone."

He heard the story of Scott's experiment a million times, but something about Sam telling him now caused a bundle of despair to burrow its way into his stomach.

"I won't let you leave." Her hair jumped in the wind like embers from a flame. "Wishville sucks, but it's all we have."

"Sure." Benji nodded, but he felt nothing. "I guess." He stepped out of the water, sand accumulating on his feet as an unreliable sock.

Sam's frown lightened as they walked away from the shore. When they reached their original spot, they sat and balanced their sodas on the sand.

"Plus," she said, "how do you plan on leaving town when your mom hardly lets you leave the house?"

"Oh, shut up." He put his socks and shoes back on, not even bothering to get rid of the sand on his feet. He wanted to remember the feeling.

"She doesn't know you came here, does she?"

"Nope, and she won't know, because *you* aren't gonna tell her." He swiped her soda from the sand and held it in front of him.

"What, you think I'm a snitch?" She reached for the can, but he pulled it away. "Seriously, Benji, I'm the one who bought it."

He laughed and returned it to her with a fading grin. Today was another awful spring festival to add to the list of memories. Another day in Wishville. Another day the same. Benji was surrounded by everyone he knew. He was sitting next to a girl who claimed to understand him. Yet for some strange reason, he had never felt less understood.

CHAPTER 4

score

James counted from one to ten in his head. When he reached ten, he counted from ten to one and back again. He repeated this endless cycle until his breathing steadied, and his nerves no longer fought him.

The classroom was the same as always. Scattered notes across the chalkboard, crumpled papers scattering the floor like confetti. Mr. Trenton leaned comfortably in his chair while the class enjoyed a five-minute beak. But although everything was normal, James could no longer focus on the book he was reading. The words scattered across his vision like an unsolved jigsaw puzzle.

He started again. *One, two, three . . .*

Most of the class didn't know it yet, but today they'd be receiving their exam scores. At the beginning of each year, before tossing away the complementary school calendar, James would find their score announcement day and mark it on his agenda. He had seen this day coming since the beginning of eighth grade, so when the Mr. Trenton established the end of their five-minute break by announcing their scores were here, James was the only one who was able to contain his panic.

"You shouldn't be nervous about them." Mr. Trenton's gaze locked on Benji, who had his head in his palms. "The exams are meant to track *progress*." He smiled at the stack of yellow papers in his hand as though they were shining blocks of gold. "As long as you did better than last year, you shouldn't be concerned."

Jett spoke as he raised his hand. "What if you *didn't* do better?"

"If that's the case, then I shouldn't let you graduate." Mr. Trenton flipped the first paper onto Noah's desk and searched for his second victim, leaving Jett with blank eyes and a billion questions buzzing through his brain. It was refreshing to see Jett concerned over grades for once. But the humor was only a temporary relief, and as the room filled with nervous whispers, James had difficulty counting.

Ten, nine, eight . . .

Soon, the time came. Mr. Trenton's stack was slender now. James glued his eyes to the page he had been reading for the last ten minutes and waited for the moment he'd been dreading all year.

An upside-down paper slid in front of him. Before deciding to look, James stuck a dime between the pages of his book and observed the room. Students were either waiting in angst or rubbing foreheads at their scores. Jett, who usually faced anywhere but the front, was sitting properly, hunched over his desk with a face hard enough to penetrate wood. Pencils rolled across desks, feet tapped, and a couple of girls in the back squealed like thirsty parrots. It's crazy how easy it was to scare children with nothing but a few scattered numbers.

Three, four, five. James flipped his paper over.

His scores had always been high enough to skip a couple of grades. Although he considered it for some time, Mr. Koi wouldn't allow him. He explained that attending school with his peers would improve his communication skills, which would prove beneficial when taking over the family businesses. His father's high expectations were affirmed in that conversation, and since then, he had put in his full effort to over-perform. It wasn't a matter of obtaining impressive scores anymore—it all narrowed to doing *better* than impressive. Each year his numbers increased. Low eighties to high eighties. High eighties to low nineties. Since they were always high, the pressure to perform better on the next test was monstrous. It was different from having mid-sixties, where with a bit of studying one could make a twenty-point jump.

This was the last year they'd be required to take the annual exam, and James was determined to end his primary school career on a successful note. He looked at the page. He read the numbers.

The room was desaturated, colorless.

Black.

All he could see were three rows in front of him, arranged in a neat chart.

Math: 98
Science: 97
English: 99

He exhaled a breath of hot air he'd been holding. High nineties—that was better than last year. He was safe.

Benji had his own paper in hand, his forehead creased as he read. After a few moments, he shut his eyes and nodded in acceptance. He wasn't a genius, or even among the smartest. Yet although James's scores from over the years were obviously favorable, Benji was Mr. Trenton's favorite student. Probably because he was always eager to raise his hand in class, which James never bothered with. Why participate if his classmates didn't care about what he had to say?

Audrey, who sat in front of James, spun around in her chair. "So," she said, "how'd it go?" Her hazel eyes shimmered, despite the room's dull light.

Everyone knew Audrey was the second-smartest person in the room. Her scores had always been only a percent or so behind James's. By the fourth grade, she was reading at a high school level and solving complex riddles in her spare time. Now she was also class president, as well as the best player on Wishville Junior High's basketball team. Sam heard from her brothers that she practiced basketball with the high school players every summer break. Sam called it cheating, but James called it resourceful.

The main talent that differentiated Audrey from James was her musical abilities through the violin, which he had no experience in whatsoever. Despite her ability to exceed in every aspect of her life, she was always humble, which drove Sam crazy. Sam had always tried to convince him that Audrey had been rivaling him all these years, but he never believed it.

Rival or not, Audrey was nice to him. He motioned to the paper with his eyes, and she rotated it. "As expected, you did amazing."

She passed him her own yellow sheet. Mid-nineties.

"I guess I did alright." Her silky hair hung from her head in thin wisps, and she spoke with a voice of soft cream. "I don't know how you do it. You're like a walking encyclopedia. But—you know—with a sense of style."

James frowned. "Thanks?"

The bell rang, and Audrey took her paper back. "Can you believe we'll be in high school soon?" She swung her mint backpack over her shoulder and took a sip from her thermos of tea. "You should have lunch with us in the music room sometime. Noah and Peyton really admire you. I mean—I do, too—of course, but really, you should. Sorry, that wasn't English."

James nodded as he slid his paper into a folder to keep it crisp. He was quick to leave the room in search of his parents. Benji must have run right after him, because *Good work* echoed down the hall. Mr. Trenton always complimented Benji's achievements, but never James's. Maybe he assumed he had enough recognition at home.

James heightened his pace, not in the mood for a chat, but he couldn't escape them. Three kids swarmed in front of him, forming a wall between James and the entrance. Sam crossed her arms, Chloe detangled a piece of hair with her fingers, and Benji's eyes glowed with a furious curiosity. James waited for them to say it. *"So what'd you get?"* It was always the same question they asked each year, and he would always answer with pride. He was preparing to share his three numbers when a new question struck him.

"What happened yesterday?" Benji stuck his hands in his sweatshirt pocket. Waiting. James understood the true intentions behind his vague question. He was trying to trip him. Trying to get him to say something he wanted to hear.

James had played this game before. He raised his stiff brows. "What do *you* think?"

Students zoomed through the halls, bumping shoulders and fleeing down the front steps. The four friends were trapped in time. Motionless in a world that wouldn't stop turning. As James waited for Benji's answer, Sam coughed, marking her participation in the game. "Enough joking around," she said. "You think we don't want an explanation?"

James remembered his parents rushing Nina to the hospital. He remembered sitting in the room, trapped between distant stars, forced to watch Earth circle the Sun. He bit his lip until it bled.

The hallways darkened. All James heard was the slamming of lockers and muttering of children. He wasn't sure how much time had passed before Sam spoke again. "We were just worried," she said. "No reason to be all sour about it."

"I don't understand these weird codes." Chloe zipped her jacket. "Is Nina okay?" There it was, the true question.

James relaxed his jaw. "It's not important."

Benji remembered the night he came home from Blueberry last week. He remembered Nina's strange apology. "Do you know something about Nina that—"

"It's an act." James tried to bite his lip again, but the tender flesh caused him to wince, so resorted to pinching his forearm. "She wants attention."

Chloe kicked the heels of her boots against the floor. "You shouldn't talk that way about her. If something happened to my sister—"

"Well your sister isn't Nina!"

James lost control of his heavy breathing. They watched him silently, trying to read him. It stayed like that for a while, the other students trickling out the entrance of the school, the intervals of time between locker slams growing increasingly larger. The tension grew to the point that James had to start counting again. One to ten, ten to one, back again.

Sam couldn't take much more of it. She broke from the group, heading to the door. "This is stupid. I'll see you idiots tomorrow."

Chloe was next. Her eyes trailed to the hallways clock, and she jumped a few times in nervous response. "Late to practice. Coach is gonna kill me." She hopped backwards away from them, waving. "Come to my funeral, will you?"

James stopped counting when he noticed the red dot he'd pinched on his arm. As he headed for the exit, Benji finally said it.

"So what'd you get?"

James stood at Nina's bedside. She sat against a tower of fluffy pillows, fidgeting with one of his wooden puzzles.

Unfazed by his appearance, she continued, her braids resting calmly on her shoulders. "I've almost got it."

James swiped it from her.

"Hey!"

He gave it a few solid turns and held the two twists of wood in both hands to show he had disconnected them properly. "Use your brain." He merged them again, gave the pieces some messing with, and tossed it back into her hands.

"Now I have to start over."

"You're welcome." James laughed at her pouting face, but eventually, she gave in and giggled with him. Nina's laugh could resurrect even the most dead colors, so James had always longed to hear it. When the colors came, she was no longer the sick one. The weird kid. The sister he had to live for. And sometimes, he wished other people could meet this girl.

But when she dropped the smile and worked on the wooden puzzle from the beginning, everything was back to normal. Back to the way they've always been. Colorless and dry. An independent, gifted student and his sick, adorable little sister.

"Hey," James said softly. "Stop the act. We both know you can't tell the future."

"Not acting."

The two stared at each other deeply, and with only a moment of eye contact, an entire argument was spoken between their heads.

"I don't understand it." James leaned back, accepting defeat. "That's all."

"It takes a special kind of person to believe me."

"Yeah. Very special." James was about to grin, but

was interrupted by the door. Mr. and Mrs. Koi peeked their heads inside to make sure Nina was awake before entering.

"How are you feeling?" Mrs. Koi rushed to Nina's bedside, forcing James to step out of the way.

"I'm fine."

While Nina battled their mom to leave her alone, the chair in the corner called for James. He threw his backpack against the wall before tossing himself onto a pile of blankets and pillows. The scent of hospital, which he hadn't noticed since he entered, filled his lungs with a scorching burn. He tasted that smell too many times, and he was sick of it. These hospital visits with Nina were always the same. A bunch of workers with fake smiles and dry hands that smelled like alcohol. No matter how many masks he layered over his mouth, the scent of hand sanitizer would never leave his nose. He reread his high numbers one last time as his dad walked toward him.

"James." Mr. Koi adjusted his glasses. "How was your day?"

"Great, we—"

"I see you spoke with Nina."

James folded his paper.

Mr. Koi knelt in front of him, lowering his voice. "Did she mention anything to you?" He watched Nina working through the wooden puzzle as Mrs. Koi rebraided her hair. "About *you know what*?"

"No." James raised the folded paper in his hand. "Today we got our . . ."

Mr. Koi faced him with shimmering eyes. His forehead was filled with mountains and valleys, his breathing uneven. Then James looked at his mother, whose hands were shaking as she ran her finger through Nina's cold hair.

Mr. Koi tilted his head as if to ask, *You were saying?*

James lowered his paper. "I'm going on a walk." He stood, allowing Mr. Koi's hand to slip off his shoulder.

"It's getting late," Mr. Koi said as he opened the door. But that was as far as he'd go to stop James from leaving.

James found himself in Wishville's town square. He wasn't sure what brought him here, but the atmosphere calmed him, so he didn't question himself.

It was quiet for a Friday. Perhaps the square had lost popularity since the last time he came, which was during last year's festival. He stopped at Ms. Camille's flower shop, observing a layer of damp cardboard taped over the broken window. *Was Jett fooling around again?* He counted five blinks before moving on.

When he reached Seaside Cafe, he leaned against the brick wall. He ensured he was far enough from the window that no one inside could see him. After a few moments of staring blankly at the courtyard fountain, listening to the water trickle from the top spout into the miniature pool below, he raised his arm and peeked at his scores again.

"I don't know how you do it."

Lauren Winchester loomed over his shoulder, wide eyes on his scores. When he was younger she was Benji's babysitter, since Rebecca was uncomfortable leaving him home alone. Lauren often had Benji's friends come over, including James. She'd give them snacks and send Benji off with them for a few hours without Rebecca's permission. She was only a high schooler at the time, and although James found her extroverted nature somewhat intimidating, he learned to appreciate her.

"Really," Lauren said, "those scores are incredible."

She was wearing her usual coffee shop uniform—khaki pants, a black collared shirt, and a plaid cross tie. When she graduated from Wishville High and started working at Seaside Cafe, James had found her uniform comical. She was always known for despising strict dress codes. In high school she launched a petition to remove the rule of wearing collared shirts to school, which was successful, yet here she was in the town square, stuck in the same quandary.

James bit the opposite side of his lip, avoiding the wound he had caused earlier. "Maybe."

"You kidding?" She undid the top button of her shirt and adjusted her collar. "When I was your age I was scoring in the thirties and forties. Well, I guess that continued in the high school exams too."

"Were you doing it intentionally?"

"Wow." Lauren shook her head, grinning. "Not all of us are from the Koi family, just so you know."

James bit his lip harder, and Lauren, sensing something was wrong, changed the subject. "Talked to my boss about the collar thing, but I don't think I was convincing enough." She straightened her crooked tie. "You haven't been here in a while, huh? Wanna get some coffee?"

"I don't drink coffee."

"Hot chocolate?"

"I don't like sweets."

Lauren pursed her lips and dropped her grin. It was a rare occurrence to witness her serious side. "Is this about your sister?" She leaned against the wall next to him. "I'm sorry you have to deal with that. It must be tough, but we can only hope—"

"Can someone stop talking about Nina for once?" His hands tensed, and he had to pinch his arm again to relax them. There was never a right time to lose his temper. Never. He knew this, yet he still spoke without control.

"My shift." The ocean in her eyes flattened. Waveless. "It's starting." She tapped her watch and was gone.

James glanced at his paper one last time. Without a thought, he crumpled it with stiff fingers and tossed it into the nearest trash bin. The sky mocked him with that same shade of gray.

For a moment he understood why Benji tried to leave Wishville. It'd be relaxing to be away from it all—to be removed from reality. Books were temporary, but leaving town was permanent.

Don't be stupid. He walked slowly to the hospital. *I miss my book.*

CHAPTER 5

mayor

When James was absent from school the next morning, Mr. Trenton's eyes shot to Benji, as if he might somehow know the answer. He only shrugged, so class began.

"Remember, the essay is due next Wednesday." Mr. Trenton paced in front of his desk, hands behind his back. "Don't procrastinate; it shows." He planted his feet, eyes locked on Jett.

Jett tucked his chin to his neck and frowned. "Why me?" He tried to maintain the angry act, but it didn't last long. Soon he broke a grin, and the class filled with laughter. Color struck the room in a flash of lightning, filling the class with a temporary rainbow. But when Benji's gaze landed on Audrey, she wasn't smiling with the rest of them.

No matter how many times she checked, the desk behind her was empty.

"I'll give you the next twenty minutes to work on your outlines." Mr. Trenton sat, then spun in his wheeled chair, grabbing a novel from his desk in the process. The class applauded him to encourage his silliness, and it worked, because he did a few extra bonus spins.

"Whoa, a bit dizzy now."

This time, Audrey faced the front and giggled. She tossed a few wisps of hair behind her shoulders and out of her eyes.

Sam nudged Benji in the side, and he hopped in his seat, eyes wide. "Seriously, Sam," he said, "that's really annoying."

"You think I care?" She leaned over the aisle and lowered her voice. "Does it have to do with Nina?"

Benji didn't have time to answer. The relaxed mood of the classroom was interrupted by a sudden swing of the door.

"Greetings!" The voice blasted through the room, and Benji recognized it instantly.

Kids whispered and raised brows at each other, shocked by Mayor Perkins' appearance. It wasn't often that he paid a visit to the schools.

"Good morning, Mayor Perkins." Audrey straightened her back. "What brings you here today?" Benji couldn't stop staring at Audrey's smile, but that wasn't what intrigued him the most. There was something special about her voice. It was smooth and warm, and whenever she spoke, goosebumps filled his arms.

"What a brat," Sam muttered.

"Polite as always, I see." Mayor Perkins smiled at Audrey before turning to Mr. Trenton. "If I may, I'd like to steal one of your students. Rest assured, I have the proper permission to do so."

"Of course, sir." Mr. Trenton smiled. "What for?"

The whispers faded.

"I'm afraid that's none of your concern." The mayor gave Mr. Trenton a pat on the shoulder, and the teacher faced his desk with a new dullness in his eyes.

The room was silent. Benji was sure that time must've stopped. He watched Audrey scribble a few words onto her teal composition notebook.

"Benji Marino."

Audrey set her pen down and glanced at Benji. His eyes widened, and he peeled his face away. *Why did she look at me?*

A sudden blow struck his side, and he shot out of his seat. He stared blankly in front of him for a moment, frozen. Sam burst into laughter, pleased with herself, and the rest of the class joined with hints of rose in their cheeks.

"Benji," Mayor Perkins said, a grin running past his face. "Would you mind coming with me?"

It was at that moment when his world crashed. Mayor Perkins had found out about his escape plan! Now he was dragging him out to school to talk to him, to lay out some kind of punishment. He'd have to think of a lie to cover it up, and fast.

But how could he know? Benji slowly craned his head to the left, staring right into Sam's eyes. He got caught in them, and he could tell she was equally as clueless. *Surely it couldn't have been James . . .*

"Benji?" Mayor Perkins stood at the door now, waiting.

"Sorry." He grabbed his backpack and followed the mayor out of the room, shooting a final glance at Sam and Chloe before the door shut for good.

Mayor Perkins walked a few feet ahead of him, and

Benji kept his distance. The more time he had to think about a cover-up to his escape, the better. But soon the mayor stopped in the middle of the hall, and his voice softened.

"I assume you know where I'm taking you?"

Benji froze. "You're . . . taking me somewhere?"

———

Benji was soon to discover that his little field trip had nothing to do with his plan to leave.

As they entered the hospital, Mrs. Koi encased Benji in a hug tight enough to choke. "Oh, I'm so glad you're here. Nina's been throwing a fit to see you." She pulled herself away, wiping her eyes with a dry finger. "Follow me."

Benji hoped Mayor Perkins would offer some kind of explanation, but the man was already making himself comfortable in the lobby's lounge.

He trailed behind Mrs. Koi, searching for a sign of James as they navigated the narrow hallways. He didn't see him until they entered a stuffy hospital room. James and Mr. Koi sat on a firm sofa in the corner, James reading a book while his father immersed himself in a newspaper. They looked at Mrs. Koi in unison, not a single expression on their faces. However, the person to catch Benji's attention was neither of them.

To the left of the room was Nina. He couldn't tell if her skin had always been that shade, or if the sun deprivation from sleeping all day had finally hit her. Either way, her normally caramel-tone had lightened to that of a roasted cashew. She was awake, leaned against a tower of pillows. Her hair wasn't in braids for once. Her scratchy locks formed a second pillow around her head.

She smiled, still yet to look at Benji. "Dad?"

He peeled himself from James's side as though it were second-nature, abandoning his newspaper. "Yes, sweetie?" Benji tried to make eye contact with James, but he remained hidden behind his book as if trapped inside it.

"Can I talk to Benji now?" Nina asked.

Mr. Koi nodded softly. "Of course."

She waited. The room was cold.

"I mean, alone?"

By the time Mr. and Mrs. Koi had figured out what Nina was trying to say, James was already halfway to the door with his book.

Mrs. Koi turned to her husband. "Are you sure that's a good idea?"

Mr. Koi walked around her and gave Benji a quick pat on the back. "Call if anything goes wrong, okay?"

And like that, the family disappeared into the hall. He took his backpack off, setting it on a chair leaned against the wall. He approached Nina's bedside, waiting.

He stared at Nina, and she stared back. Her eyes yielded that same void, deep enough to suck anyone into them. Two miniature black holes.

"Benji." She sat straighter in the hospital bed and gulped. "I'm sorry." Her eyes drooped so much that Benji tried to think of a way to stop her from crying. But she didn't.

"I wanted to say goodbye."

At first it didn't make sense, but after repeating the sentence a few times in his head, the news sunk in. Benji stepped closer to the bed. The air reeked of that bitter hospital smell. Toothpaste and alcohol. "Goodbye?"

"My health has never been good, you know that." Nina stared through the crack between the tightly drawn curtains. "It's going to fail soon."

"Fail?"

"I'll be gone by six in the morning."

Benji's hands went stiff, but he controlled his breathing. "Is that what the doctor told you?"

She shook her head. "I know."

Benji's stomach churned, but he forced the feeling away and smiled. "You'll be fine. You don't know that." For some reason, it was painful.

"I know about you, too." She blinked. "I know how you tried to leave Wishville that day."

Benji gulped. "James told you?"

"Why would he?"

She was right. Unless there was some kind of benefit involved, James would never speak a word of it.

"I wanted to say sorry." She reached under a pillow next to her, searching for something. "There's nothing I can do to help."

"What—what are you—"

"Do you want to know?" Her smile disappeared.

Benji's arms turned to boards. "Know what?"

She stared at him blankly, as if he might be joking. "When you'll die."

His breathing stuttered. He took a few steps back, recalling the strange events in order.

"It's been bothering me lately," she said. "How people are unable to prepare for their passing."

Benji collapsed onto a stiff chair against the wall. "I don't know." He stared at the ground and shut his eyes. "Please, I really don't know."

"You don't need to decide now." Pulling her arm out from under the pillow, she held red envelope toward him with a frail arm. "Open it when you're ready."

His eyes twinkled naturally, and he stood, heading toward it. Something about red was oddly attractive. His hands trembled as he reached for the envelope.

"Why so nervous?" Nina tilted her head as he took it. "It's a good opportunity. You can make reasonable plans."

"Reasonable?"

Nina bit her lip.

But then Benji remembered that he was in a hospital room, and that Nina had been taken to visit a psychologist. He remembered seeing how worried Mr. and Mrs. Koi were over Nina. He remembered that she was ill. Benji took one last breath before straightening his back and strengthening his voice. "Nina, you can't tell the future, and you're not gonna die." He smiled and glanced at the clock. "When you're feeling better, I'll visit you."

She stared at her lap, her face buried behind her hair. "Okay."

Benji lifted the envelope, and a ghostly chill passed through him. Goosebumps filled his arms as he slipped on his backpack, trying to forget. He smiled at her one last time and left the room without turning back.

The town square was the only place in town where the smell of clam and coffee was pungent enough that the air no longer reeked of saltwater and seagulls.

Every time Benji went to the square he'd experience a little knot of excitement because *something* had changed. Maybe it was a new mat in front of the bookstore, or a few unfamiliar flowers peeking through the window of Ms. Camille's shop. Even the little things made Benji's heart flutter.

"I hope Rebecca doesn't mind me taking you here on the way home." Mayor Perkins led Benji toward the coffee shop with that same enchanting smile of his. "When we were younger, your dad and I would sometimes have coffee together. She was always against it." He held the door open for Benji and followed in after him. "You see, our parents didn't let us have coffee, so we'd go all out when we could. Sea salt caramel mocha with two shots of espresso. Just about the most caffeinated drink you can get in town."

Benji smiled. "Yeah?"

The room filled with light as customers set eyes on the mayor. The only person to notice the short kid next to him was Lauren.

She leaned over the counter. "Got yourself a new babysitter, I see." There was a blob of white goop in her hair.

"Uh—Lauren—"

"I know, I know." She rolled her eyes and pointed a thumb to a guy in the corner, dressed in a matching uniform. "All Ricky's fault. Didn't know how a whipped cream pump worked."

Ricky looked up from the milk steamer. "Hey!"

The mayor appeared behind Benji, and Lauren straightened her posture. "Good evening, Mayor Perkins." She smiled with as little evil as she could handle. "What can I get for you today?"

"Two sea salt caramel mochas." He grinned at Benji. "Double shots of espresso."

Lauren wrote a few notes on a paper pad. "Trying to shorten the kid down, I see."

Benji tried not to laugh, but he couldn't help it.

"Gotta give him a sense of freedom." He shook Benji by the shoulder until his brain was fried. "Am I right?"

Seaside Cafe was known for the warm interior atmosphere, unlike Chowdies, where practically everything was white. The cafe was painted in dark oranges and reds, had black molding around the windows, and was filled with wooden tables crafted in a variety of styles out of different types of woods.

They sat in the corner by the window. The table was made of old mahogany with a smooth matte finish. Benji ran his hand along the wood as he watched the ocean dance outside the window. The waves were everywhere, and Benji was sick of it.

"We'd sit here in this very seat." Mayor Perkins smiled widely. "Ah, I remember those days."

There was a question that had been on his mind for a while. A question he'd never dare ask Rebecca. But as he sat with Mayor Perkins, admiring the atmosphere, the timing felt right. "My dad," Benji said. "Why would he choose to do the experiment? Why not someone else? Someone without a family?"

"No one fully understands it." Mayor Perkins tapped his fingers on the table. "But I guess you could say he had the right nature for it. He was always trying new things. Taking risks, no matter the consequences. Probably the most creative kid in school. And look where it got him." He shut his eyes. "Got him killed."

Lauren slipped the drinks in front of them, lightening the tone. "Enjoy your sugar bombs."

"No need to tell me how many grams are in this thing." Mayor Perkins lifted the cup as a sign of thanks.

"No need to worry." Lauren winked. "Only 97."

She left, leaving a look of disgust across the mayor's face. But that wasn't enough to stop him from drinking it. He took a sip, set the cup down, and stared at the ceiling with sparkling eyes. "Brings back memories."

Benji couldn't keep his mind from throbbing. "Why didn't you stop him?"

The mayor took another sip. "Hmm?"

"My dad."

"Oh, right." He set the cup down, a smile emerging across his face. "Scott was the most stubborn person I knew. When he told me he wanted to leave town, I knew there was nothing I could do to change his mind. Plus, we needed to find out if leaving town really was dangerous, or if people were simply choosing not to return. When Scott came up with a way to test it, I was both excited and terrified. I was scared of losing my best friend, but there was nothing we could do to convince him out of it. He was the most stubborn guy I knew.

Even as kids the three of us were always trying to keep him out of trouble."

Benji was about to take his first sip, but he set the cup down with a slam. "Three of you?" Benji knew Rebecca was childhood friends with Scott and Mayor Perkins. That they were a trio—that's what his mom had always said.

"She didn't tell you, huh?" He leaned over the table, as if it'd somehow keep other people in the room from hearing. "I'm not sure if you've ever heard of Oliver."

Benji shook his head.

"Oliver Stricket?"

Benji repeated the name a few times before it struck him. Oliver Stricket! The man up on the hill, Stricket! Yes, he'd heard of him. After Scott left town, Stricket moved to an abandoned house on Eudora Hill, only leaving every other Sunday night for his stop at the convenience store in the square. No one knew where his money came from. No one dared to speak to him.

"Stricket was . . . your friend?"

"Gosh, I forgot how sweet this was." Mayor Perkins took another sip. "Have you tried it yet?"

Benji raised the cup to his lips. The salt of the caramel was not strong enough to combat against the strong taste of chocolate. Then there was the coffee. This thing was strong. He could feel it buzz right to his brain. A full cup of this and he'd be jumping off the walls.

The two of them looked at each other, set their cups on the table, and laughed. Bend-over-all-the-way kind of laughs. There was no more conversation about Scott. No mentions of Stricket. But the questions never left Benji's mind.

CHAPTER 6

coffee

It wasn't until the evening of the following day when Benji heard the news. Rebecca slid a bowl from Chowdies in front of him, but he continued tapping the table in anticipation. Normally Fridays were filled with excitement for that final bell to ring. But today, he had dreaded going home. The entire school day had been a waiting game.

But this game was quick to end.

"I got a call." Rebecca sat next to him. She stuck a spoon into her bowl, tossing bits of clam around before finally raising her pale face. "Nina passed away this morning."

She watched him as his chowder grew cold. "Benji?"

He stood from the table, leaving his bowl untouched.

"I'm not hungry."

"Benji, I—"

He rushed to his room, slammed the door, and leaned against the wall with gritted teeth. Rage swept through his bones, leaving his blood boiling. He wanted to be sad. He wanted to sink to the floor in tears for such a loss, or at least for a best friend's loss. But instead, he was petrified.

His eyes shot to the red envelope, sitting crisply on his desk. *If Nina really did predict her death,* he thought, *then what does this mean for me?* He lifted the envelope. Staring at the red in his hands, he remembered the minimal times he spent with Nina. All the dinners they had with her silence at the Koi household. All the times he saw her leave her bedroom after napping through the day. All the times she threw out her food. Not hungry.

How long had she known about her death?

If only he could have one last conversation. To sit in front of her and ask if she was okay. If she was really able to handle the stress of all the knowledge resting on her shoulders. No one could guess how much she knew. How many thoughts haunted her mind.

He shut his eyes, thinking back to how calm she was when she announced her death. She laid there in the hospital that day, sharing the news like inviting him for tea. So calm. So accepting.

Biting his lip, he leaned over and jammed the envelope into the bottom drawer of his desk. "No." He slammed the drawer shut. "I won't do that to myself."

It was Sunday now. The sweet aroma of melted caramel encased him as the door shut, trapping him in the brick building. Seaside Cafe was unusually dark today. The only source of light was a hint of gray sky through one tiny window by the back entrance, where Mayor Perkins and he sat only three days ago.

"Well, look who it is!" Lauren messed with his hair until it covered his face. Benji let her joke around for a while, but eventually stepped back and flicked his hair away from his face, revealing two clouded eyes. He stared at Lauren as she laughed, but his thoughts were somewhere else. When she saw his face, her humor died. "Sit down," she said, scurrying to the other side of the room. "It's on the house today."

Benji took a seat at the nearest table. There was no one else in the room, but it made sense. He couldn't imagine how anyone would be in the mood for coffee, considering the cafe was in the heart of town, Wishville's social spot.

How are Sam and Chloe taking the news?

Lauren slid a stubby cup in front of him and stepped back with her hands on her hips, grinning. Benji watched the fluid dance in the cup.

He wrapped his fingers around the handle and took a sip. Bitter.

"This is coffee."

She messed with his hair from above once again, and when Benji swatted her hand away, immediately slipped into the seat across from him. Relentless, that girl. "Threw an extra shot in there, too." She winked. "Plus, what's the harm? I bet that drink the other day permanently stunted you."

"Why?" The smooth coffee slipped down his throat, and for a moment, although brief, his thoughts of Nina drifted away.

"I've known you forever." Lauren chuckled. "Of

course I know you have a chocolate allergy. What else is there to drink?"

"*Had.*" Benji took a large gulp. It stung his throat. "I grew out of that six years ago."

"Well I know you like coffee more than hot chocolate, so there." She raised her chin with a hint of pride in her eyes. "Plus, you look like you just crawled out of bed."

"Lauren!" It was Ricky, standing behind the cash register with shaky hands. "You're not gonna help me here?"

Lauren rolled her eyes. "Oh, shut up. There's not even a line." She turned back to Benji, waiting for some kind of response. When she didn't get one, she spoke anyway. "Hey, I know why you're here."

"You do?"

"Of course. What better place to gloom than an old coffee shop by the shore?"

"I—well—I don't think I'll be ready to go back to school tomorrow."

"Ah, I remember those days." She set her elbow on the table and gazed through the corner of her eyes. "Procrastinating on school projects. All-nighters." She shook her head, laughing gently. "I'm sure glad I'm finally out of high school."

Benji sighed. *Here she goes.*

"You think eighth grade is hard?" She laughed. "Wait until you have finals and midterms. High school sucks."

"We already do."

"Like they're *actually* challenging." Lauren rubbed her forehead. "Oh gosh. To think we considered them a big deal back then." She looked at the ceiling, water in her eyes. "High school was fun. As soon as you're a freshman you'll realize how lame middle school is."

Her words struck something inside him, and he didn't know why. The color drained from his face.

"Sorry, not the right time."

"That's not it."

When he looked at her, Lauren's blue eyes whipped around like the ocean waves, searching for answers. Perhaps that was one thing they had in common.

"It's nothing." Benji stood. "Thanks for the coffee."

Lauren leaned over the table, eyeing his cup. "You hardly touched it."

Benji paused, staring at his cup. His eyes watered, but he quickly blinked the moisture away. "I think I should've stayed home today. Sorry."

"Right." Her voice was dull. "Tell Rebecca I said hi."

"Sure."

"And Benji?"

He peeked over his shoulder, hand on the door. "Yeah?"

"Try not to think too hard. I guarantee you're not the only one stuck in the past this weekend."

Benji tried his best to pull a smile. His heart twinged as the tips of his lips came to a curve, and there was nothing more relieving than dropping it after Lauren gave him a thumbs up and headed back behind the counter.

He couldn't remember the last time he left Seaside Cafe unsatisfied. Lauren had always known the right things to say to cheer him up. He had always come to the coffee shop to get advice, or simply to calm his mind, but today, even that wouldn't work. And as much as he tried to convince himself that he could find a magic potion, a blow that would instantly remove all kinds of stress, he knew there was no such thing. He'd have to deal with this himself. All of it.

Benji was still trapped in thought when he saw him.

The man's hair curled over his head like little whips of cream, shaking with each step. He walked on his feet lightly, but there was a heaviness in his eyes that weighed him. He stopped on the pathway lining the courtyard, waiting for Benji to pass.

Oliver Stricket. The town crazy man.

Since Benji hardly came to the square on Sundays, it'd been years since he last saw him. The last time was around three years ago, during a trip for dinner at Chowdies. He remembered how Rebecca nodded at Oliver without a smile.

He was afraid of the man. After hearing the stories of his high school fights and crazy beliefs, Benji titled him psycho. But as he passed him today, he couldn't bring himself to imagine him as the same man in the stories.

Seeing that Benji was not inclined to move aside, Oliver stepped around him.

Benji was unable to peel his eyes away. Unable to blink. He watched the man pull his wrist to his chin to read the time, his silver watch sparkling in the gloom of the clouds. As he walked by, Benji spun and faced his back. He opened his mouth to speak as the distance between them grew, but his throat was deserted.

The words refusing to leave him, Benji continued on his way home.

CHAPTER 7

kois

I t came too early.

He had seen it coming from miles away. Nina had always been a clock ticking toward her own destruction. It was simply unfortunate luck that the clock broke before reaching its end.

James held the pages tightly in front of him. His favorite book, but all he could see was a mash of random letters scattered across the page. One giant blur. His breathing heightened, and he leaned over, thrusting the book across the room. It slapped the wall before landing on the floor where it remained.

Silence.

For a while he sat there in bed, watching the book as if it might move. He wished he could be frozen. That the world could stop for a moment. It was only Friday when he understood the strength of time. How it controlled him. Locked a tight grip around his neck and made the air hard to breathe, but never too hard to kill him. He was another kid trapped in a world ruled by time. Dependent on it.

And it was sickening.

He gulped, then stepped out of bed. The floor nearly burned his feet with its coldness. Each step shot chills through his spine. He remembered all the fun moments with his best friends. All the time spent on his puzzles. Reading at the dinner table. He remembered school. He remembered his scores.

"I thought I was such a genius." James reached for the door knob. It made himself freeze, so he stood there in the dark room. One hand urging him to leave, the other trying to drag him back to bed. "I knew she didn't have much time left. But I ignored it. I ignored it, thinking it might go away." He took his hand off the doorknob and rubbed his face hard. His eyes were sore, bruised. He leaned against the door and let his breath stutter.

"Of all people," James said. "Why her?"

He saw the book again, sitting there on the floor. *Sharpner's Peak*. The book that with a quick touch could extract him from reality. Every time he'd open those pages in silence, the world would stop spinning. It'd be him, alone, stuck in a universe where he wasn't constantly struggling between selfishness and understanding. He didn't have to think about Nina. He didn't have to think about his scores.

A knock came from the door, and he stumbled away from it. His breathing went from a simple unsteadiness into a rapid fire as it swung open.

Mr. Koi stood in the doorway. There was no suit. No tie. He had on a pair of plain khaki shorts and a shirt James hadn't seen him wear in years. He looked at James, heard his boy's breathing, removed his glasses, and rubbed his eyes.

That's when James saw how red they were. The man he looked up to. The man who taught him how to read before his peers could even recognize a letter. The man who taught him the weight of words. The man who taught him not to cry from insensitive remarks. That same man. But he was crying.

He took a deep step forward and wrapped his arms around James. He was warm, and James could hear his heart beating.

"Hey." Mr. Koi tightened his grip. "I'm sorry."

CHAPTER 8

school

The challenge wasn't handling the death of a child. It was facing the friends of a boy whose world had been struck by a meteor.

Chloe pulled the hood of her sweatshirt over her head. She couldn't remember the last time she'd worn one. Fourth grade, maybe.

Mr. Trenton spoke in a monotone voice, the room as colorless as ever. She traced her fingers along the shapes she had pencil-carved into her desk. All she could hear clearly was a faint scraping of chalk against the board, some muttering about parts of speech, and that was it. At some point in the lesson she remembered Mr. Trenton's strict rule about not wearing hoods in class, but she couldn't bring herself to take it off.

Benji was only a few desks away, arms as stiff as boards. He fidgeted with his own fingers, as though working his way through a hard decision. For a moment he looked back at her. His gray eyes darkened, to the point where they almost looked black from the gloom of the class. He dragged them away.

Sam, on the other hand, had her musical theory

workbook spread out in front of her. Normally she'd work on it whenever she was bored in class, not because she enjoyed it, but because she'd rather not fall behind Audrey. But today, she had trouble doing anything more than stare at the notes. Her hands rested over the page, eyes watering. Jett turned around in his seat.

"Hey," he whispered at her. When Sam didn't look at him, Jett turned to Chloe with a frown. "Is she seriously not over it yet?"

Chloe stopped admiring her desk carvings. "Are you stupid?" It took a lot to make Chloe raise her voice, yet she did it today without even realizing it.

Mr. Trenton's mumbling came to a halt, and his chalk froze over the board. The perfect opportunity for Jett to raise his voice.

"Wow, Mortimer getting all feisty today." He leaned back in his seat. "I don't get the gloom this morning. He's a lucky kid. I mean, what's a man gotta do to get some time off school?"

Sam dropped her pen. She snatched Jett by the hair and jerked his neck back.

"What the—" He rubbed the back of his neck and shot her a twisted look. "What was *that* for?"

Chloe leaned forward. "You act like you don't care!"

Jett slid his chair further from Sam, guarding his back closely. "Well it's not like I knew the girl."

"So what?" Peyton's hair was almost as frizzy as Sam's today.

"It's not just Nina." Audrey turned from her spot in the corner. Her eyes were red. "It's James."

Jett chuckled. "You think I'm friends with James?"

"Really, dude?" Noah said. "Really, you choose to argue at a time like this?"

Benji's fingers froze into fists. "Toxic," he muttered.

"Oh, you wanna go *there*, Marino!"

Sam slammed a hand on her desk. "When do you learn to shut up?"

Jett shook his head with a slight tilt of his lips. "Wow." He rolled his eyes. "Wow guys, I'm not your personal punching bag." Something about his voice was softer this time.

Noah frowned. "That's not the—"

"Enough!" The chalk slipped to the floor as Mr. Trenton spun to face the students. Each breath of his filled the room, and silence fell immediately. Chloe stared at her desk carvings once more, her cheeks growing red. She started this.

"I've heard enough. From all of you." Mr. Trenton threw himself back into his chair. "Study hall."

Jett frowned. "But class hardly even—"

"For goodness' sake, find something to work on!" He leaned over his desk and ran tense fingers through his hair. "And Chloe?"

"Yeah?"

"Take off your hood."

It was a silent day. Chloe had spent the entirety of it in a half-asleep kind of daze. Their morning study hall morphed into a period of mourning, lunch a room of children ignoring their hunger, and a final class a lesson no one could stomach.

Jett didn't speak again. Not once. And by the time the final bell rang, he was out the door before anyone else.

Chloe biked home, the salty wind ruffling her hair, the distant crashing of the waves into the sand. Her mind was dark and empty, like the house was when she arrived.

She heated a bowl of chowder and sat at the dining room table, listening to the house hum. Sometimes she liked to imagine that the place was singing.

It was the same as every night. Chloe waiting for her sister, their home silent and dimly lit. Watching the clock's hour arms slowly reach for the ten.

The chowder was warm.

She stuck her spoon back into the bowl, her eyes wandering to the photos on the wall in front of her. The first was a photo of her parents' wedding. They stared into each other's eyes, madly in love, confident their love would last until the end of time.

There was no one waiting at home for her. Not anymore. No one asking how her day went, or what she learned in school. All she had was an overworked, exhausted sister. A sister who cared for her so much that she spent nearly every waking hour away from her.

Chloe shifted her focus to the photo next to it. She stood next to Benji in the middle, James and Sam on opposite sides of them. It was from first grade, when Chloe's father asked for a photo of them all together during the spring festival.

"You four are so cute," Mr. Mortimer had said with stars in his eyes.

Chloe wasn't smiling, embarrassed that her father was snapping photos of everything. Photos of people without their permission. Photos of trees. Photos of the ocean. Photos of random cicadas clinging to bricks. He brought his camera everywhere and used it on everything.

Next to Chloe, Benji had his hands on his bare arms because he forgot to bring a jacket. Or maybe he wanted to make the day more interesting at the cost of comfort. Sam stood a weird distance from Benji, as straight as a brick, her smile too light to notice. James, on the other side of Chloe, was laughing, not because he was enjoying his time, but because a character in the book he was reading a moment ago tipped his humor.

Losing her father struck her life like a meteor. It left her family broken and burned to smoking ash. It changed her. And if it weren't for her friends, she wasn't sure how she'd survive.

The three of them were family to her. She cared for them more than anyone, and she'd never wish on them what she went through. She'd never wish them a meteor, no matter what.

Her eyes locked on James's smile as she took a last bite.

The chowder was cold.

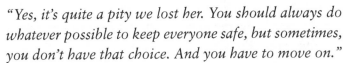

"Yes, it's quite a pity we lost her. You should always do whatever possible to keep everyone safe, but sometimes, you don't have that choice. And you have to move on."

A knock at the door.

Sam dropped her backpack on the floor and collapsed onto her bed. "Not hungry," she said to the ceiling.

"It's Tobias." She didn't respond, hoping he might

disappear. But soon the door swung open, and Tobias stepped inside. "Hey." He shut the door behind him softly. "Don't listen to what Dad said. He can be insensitive sometimes."

Sam sat and slammed her feet on the floor. "It's like he doesn't even care."

"He's the mayor, Sam." Tobias sat next to her. "He needs to look forward."

Sam stared into his far-reaching eyes. Through them she could see a man standing on the stage of the courtyard. A hand in the air, his mouth open wide. It was Tobias's dream to take over Dad's job as the mayor someday. He had known this since he was little. Always dressed the same as Dad with his fancy collared shirts tucked into his pants. Ate the same foods. Laughed at the same time. Copied that same, fake smile.

"Well unlike you, I hate being part of this family."

He frowned. "Don't say that."

"Already said it." Sam crossed her arms. "One day you'll realize that Dad isn't the perfect man you see him to be. Sure, he's the mayor, but he's still like us. He's still human."

Tobias stared at the wall. For a while he didn't say a word, and Sam was confident she won her made-up battle. But eventually, he took a deep breath and spoke.

"I never knew the girl." He didn't look at her. "But I do admit that I'm sorry for the kid."

"James?"

"Yeah."

"Me too." Sam folded her hands on her lap. "When he comes back, what do I do?"

Tobias rubbed his temple. "I think you need to keep things as normal as possible. Make him comfortable."

"Sounds rough."

"Well if anyone can do it, it's you." Tobias stood, then turned back with a wide grin. "Oh yeah, Mom says you've got dish duty tonight."

"That was *your* deal."

"Finals, Sam." He waved over his shoulder. "Gotta study."

"That's two weeks away."

"Classes are hard, sis." He slipped out the door with a grin.

"*Sure.*"

Sam sat alone in her empty room. She tried to remember what Tobias had said. That Mayor Perkins was simply thinking forward. But as hard as she tried, she couldn't get his words to leave her mind.

Sometimes, you don't have that choice. Sam wrapped her arms around her knees and took a deep breath. *And you have to move on.* She shook her head. *Move on. Move on. Move—*

"How the hell do I do that?"

The lights were still glowing at their brightest, but world darkened in her eyes. She glanced at the violin on her desk before slipping off the bed.

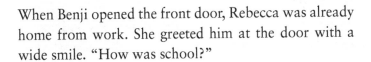

When Benji opened the front door, Rebecca was already home from work. She greeted him at the door with a wide smile. "How was school?"

He slipped off his shoes and silently walked past her.

"I have an idea." She chased after him. "Why don't we eat out tonight for a change?"

Benji paused, glancing over his shoulder. "I'm not hungry."

"I know this is a hard time for you." She sighed. "But you have to eat. It'll make you feel better. Come on, let's go! Put on your shoes."

"Sorry." Benji continued through the hall. "I'm not going."

His room was as messy as ever, but he was pleased to be back. He hopped onto his bed to lay down, staring at the ceiling above. *Why am I not sad?* After turning onto his side, he narrowed his eyes at the envelope. He snatched it from his desk and held it in front of him. *Is it because of you?*

The truth was right in his fingertips. The date of his death was only a few rips away. He wanted to know so badly. And he considered the possibility that maybe opening it would help him move on from his curiosity. Maybe it would help him. A couple of rips. That's all it would take. His grip on the envelope increased, and the room grew cold.

"Open it when you're ready." That's what Nina had told him. *"It's a good opportunity. You can make reasonable plans for your future."*

"What did she mean by that?" Benji sat and tossed his feet over the edge of the bed. "And ready? How will I know when I am?"

The door busted open, and Rebecca stood in the entryway with stiff eyes. "I'm okay with you processing all of this, but I need you to eat." Her eyes dropped to the red envelope in his hands. "What's that?"

"Oh, it's a—you know—birthday party invitation."

She frowned. "From who?"

"Jett." Benji bit his lip.

"That's odd. He doesn't usually invite you, does he?"

"Not really." Benji tossed it onto his desk as if it were an old bill. "I don't think I feel like going."

Something about Rebecca's face suddenly softened. She sat herself next to Benji and wrapped an arm around him. "You don't have to deal with this alone, okay?" She took a deep breath. "I know what it's like to lose someone. And I know it's especially hard when the people around you are struggling, too."

His body went numb as he clenched his eyes shut. He wanted to tell her, *No, that's not why I'm upset.* As much as it hurt knowing Nina was gone, the envelope never left his head. That stupid envelope! Whispering for him to come back. Haunting him.

Nina could tell the future. That was the only explanation that made sense to him. And maybe if he opened the envelope, he'd reach some kind of understanding. Maybe that envelope was the missing piece to the puzzle. But at the same time, was he going insane? No one believed in Nina's crazy stories. She was a sick girl with a strong imagination, but was that really the truth?

It sounded a lot like that rumor about Stricket. He remembered hearing something about the man seeing a . . . what was it? A ghost? A foreign face? He couldn't remember, but he did know that the story was oddly familiar. A boy no one believed in. A boy who claimed the impossible.

"Mom?" Benji looked at her and frowned. "Why didn't you ever tell me you three were friends with Stricket?"

All traces of color left her face. She stared for a while, deep into his eyes, then shook her head gently. "Who told you that?"

"The mayor, Mom." Benji looked back at the floor. "I remember these rumors about him being involved in some kind of supernatural... paranormal... I don't know. But what if it was all true? What if he was like Nina? What if it's really *us* who can't understand their—"

"Benji!" She grabbed his shoulder and waited for him to look at her. "I won't hear any more of this Oliver nonsense."

"I was—"

"Why don't you eat something?" She lightened her grip on his shoulder and smiled. "It might help you think straight."

CHAPTER 9

cafeteria

"It's good to have you back." Mr. Trenton did his best to pull a genuine smile, only receiving a short nod in return.

James was late. Thirty-two minutes late, exactly. But that didn't seem to matter. It didn't matter to Mr. Trenton, and it certainly didn't matter to the rest of the class. Everyone was more focused on his presence than his timing. Everyone except for Benji.

He didn't smile at James. Didn't look at him. He knew he should do *something*, but he couldn't imagine what would be considered acceptable, so instead, he stared at his desk with frozen eyes.

Stares radiated past Benji in James's direction. A rain of curious eyeballs. He heard Mr. Trenton plop onto his chair and roll to his desk, ending the lecture. Even he must have been staring.

Everyone waited for James to do something marvelous. After all, it was easier to react than be the actor. Today, James stood in the gold spotlight. He was the star of the play, and the star wasn't moving.

So they waited.

James hadn't spoken since he entered, and hadn't moved since he sat. Benji gathered the courage to glance at him, hoping he wouldn't notice, and he didn't. He looked the same as he always had. Same stylish clothes. Same haircut. Everything was the same.

But it didn't feel right.

He moved his hand, leading the class to flinch in unison, but he had only reached to rub his eyes. It hadn't even been a week yet. Had he come too early? Too late? How long was too late?

Benji folded his hands together. He wanted to think about James. He wanted to welcome him back to school. To see how he was doing. But his mind was too muddled to think. The envelope flashed in his mind, but he tucked the image away. He was stuck in constant war with himself, his brain refusing to grant peace.

Sam leaned over the aisle. "You okay?"

Benji faced the opposite wall. He could see her watching him from the corner of his eye, but eventually, she looked away.

"Jeez, what's with the weather?" Jett turned sideways in his seat, facing the class. He made eye contact with Benji for a moment and smiled. It wasn't his usual rancid display of teeth. It was gentle, a slight bend of his lips. Jett wasn't clueless this time. He was trying to break the tension.

The students sheltered their eyes. If they caught another soul's gaze, they'd drag their chin in all directions until no one was in sight. Human eye contact was enough to kill. Even a hushed voice was poisonous.

But slowly, the eyes grew more comfortable. Benji heard Noah and Peyton whispering behind him. A light chattering filled the room, and he was grateful for it. The stiffness in the air tossed away, and with the loss of it came a casual attraction to James. No more vicious stares. No more vile silence.

Audrey spun around, facing James. "Hey."

James looked at her blankly.

"Wanna have lunch with us in the music room today?"

Benji heard Sam huff, and for the first time, he didn't judge her for it. How many times would Audrey ask him? James never replied. Every time, he was silent. Maybe Audrey thought she had the power to change his mind, but James's brain was not a place easily tampered with.

James reached into his backpack, retrieving *Sharpner's Peak*, and Benji squinted at the corner. One of the bottom corners was smashed into a wrinkly dent. An odd observation, considering James had always treated the book with intensive care.

He opened his book, but his eyes were on Audrey. The room brightened, the blinding blue reflection of the ocean washing through the window and into the classroom air. James smiled at her, and this time, he spoke.

"Maybe next time."

The cafeteria was gray.

Benji ran his hand along their favorite lunch table. He knew the cafeteria tables were forest green, but no matter how hard he stared at them today, he couldn't see it. A blurry fog filled his vision, mushing all the different colors of the room together until it no longer had a color. Although he couldn't see the other middle schoolers eating, he could hear them. He could hear everything. The chewing, the chattering, the smacking of lips.

Chloe's tuna sandwich had too much mayonnaise—Benji could tell by the way it squished as she bit into it. Sam ignored her strawberry soda, tapping her fingers against the table, humming a song that had been stuck on her mind all week. The notes filled Benji's mind, mixing with the noises of food. The eating. The talking. The gulping.

The vibrations of Sam's tapping on the table stopped. "What's going on with you today?"

Benji raised his chin away from the table, searching for Sam's face, but his focus redirected to James. Besides their love for puzzles and reading, James and Nina had nothing in common. But today, as Benji looked at his friend, all he could see was Nina. A face draining of color, a mask of bulletproof skin.

Benji rubbed his eyes—and Nina turned back into James. The sounds of the room intensified.

I have to ask him.

He slammed his eyes shut. The darkness overpowered the bright colors and sounds shooting through his brain.

"Last night, I almost did it." Benji's head flashed with a screen of blood red, but it happened so quickly he assumed the color was his imagination.

Chloe set her sandwich down. "Did what?"

The confidence flooded back to him, allowing the

words to flow. "James," Benji said. "Did Nina ever talk to you about the future?"

James didn't flinch. He was a statue, frozen. But Benji could tell by the weird slant of his lips that he was biting them.

"Seriously, Benji?" Sam wrapped her hand around her soda, but she still didn't drink it. "Are you stupid?"

James's lip fell normal as he dropped his jaw to speak. "You fell for the act."

"I didn't fall," Benji said. "I believed."

"What are you guys talking about?" Chloe tapped her foot repeatedly against the floor, and Benji had a hard time tuning out the subtle taps.

"She gave me an envelope with my future and it— it's driving me crazy!" The table shifted from gray to red, and he yanked his hand away. The table was hot. Burning. He felt the heat dissipate as the color morphed back into its usual green. "I can't stop thinking about what she had to go through, and that I might—"

"That's funny." James's mouth smiled, but his eyes didn't. "My sister dies and she's still the topic of discussion."

The room darkened as James slid out of the bench, abandoning his cafeteria tray. He didn't wave. He didn't say goodbye.

"James?" The cafeteria sounds rumbled through his head, but he couldn't hear himself. He was calling clearly, but no one was listening. Every word that left his lips drowned in the busy air, and for some absurd reason, he thought of Nina.

"Wow, great job." Sam pointed to the cafeteria door.

"Why the heck would you do that? He literally just came back. We should be acting *normal*."

Chloe packed her sandwich back into the bag, no longer planning to eat it. "She has a point."

Benji flicked the hair out of his face. "I've been confused lately."

"You're not confused, you idiot." Sam raised her chin, pouring a stream of soda into her mouth. After a large gulp, her face went red. "You're *curious*. Don't you get it? This is the kind of stuff that happens when you keep asking all your stupid questions."

"There's no such thing as stupid questions."

"Cute. Is that what your dad used to tell you?"

Chloe formed her hair into a ponytail. "Both of you, calm down."

"You know what? Why don't you pack your things and go find Scott?" Sam leaned toward him, lowering her voice. "I won't stop you this time."

"Hey, careful." Chloe searched the room. "Someone could hear."

"You don't know when to stop, do you?" Benji stared at Sam's fiery hair, his blood simmering.

"Me? I don't know when to stop? James needs us right now, but you had to go and make a mess, like you always do." She tossed her empty soda can into the closest trash bin and put her backpack on. "I'm gonna find him."

Chloe had just put her hair in a ponytail when she took it down again. A few strands fell over her face like clean cuts in soft skin. "Sam, don't."

But it was too late. Sam stormed to the hall, each step louder than the last. The cafeteria exploded with whispers, and a group of seventh-graders tried to contain their laughter in the center of the room. They had probably been watching the scene since the beginning, considering James was the center of attention today. Benji had been too trapped in his own world to notice. Too trapped to notice anything, apparently.

"Hey, don't worry too much." The corner of Chloe's lips tilted upward, a slight indication of what was meant to be a smile. "I'm sure they'll both get over it. But try to be more—you know—careful next time."

CHAPTER 10

dinner

Apparently Benji's luck was not ready to kick in. Mayor Perkins had invited him and Rebecca for dinner—the last place he'd like to spend his evening. He still didn't know how he'd face Sam after what happened at lunch.

It was the first time Benji second-guessed his clothes in a while. It hadn't occurred to him until later in the afternoon that he had been wearing no more than two different outfits since the day Nina died. Not only that, but they were also all the same color scheme of plaid. He switched into a sweatshirt collecting dust in the corner of his room and slipped a few pennies into his pocket for good luck.

They left the house at six thirty. It probably would have been six, had Benji not been stalling. "I don't get why you're in such a bad mood today." Rebecca locked her hands on the steering wheel. "I thought you loved going to the mayor's place."

Benji shrugged and stared out the window for the remainder of the trip.

Mrs. Perkins was the one to answer the door. Her

white dress hugged her waist and billowed elegantly around her ankles. Most would argue that she was the most elegant woman in town—always pinning her hair in fancy designs and reapplying moisturizer throughout the day. Benji almost wished his mom was as youthful as the mayor's wife. Rebecca was already showing signs of age, and she was younger than most mothers in Wishville. She also worked harder.

Sam had three brothers, all older than her. One was a senior in high school, and the other two were twins prepping for their junior year. Benji looked up to them. He always wished he had a brother. Or a sister, even. That wouldn't be all that bad. But it was just him. Just Benji.

"So nice to see you." Mrs. Perkins set her hands on her cheeks and stepped aside. Her voice went from high to low pitch as she talked, something that seemed to ensnare all she spoke to. She must have adopted her charm from the mayor.

Food was always interesting at the Perkins' place. Sitting on the table was a heavy bowl of pesto pasta, Benji's favorite, accompanied with salad and garlic bread. It was rare to find such a meal in Wishville, where all people cared about were clams and fish and seaweed. He wondered why no one hunted seagulls. Those pests were everywhere.

Benji sat between Rebecca and the mayor's oldest son, Tobias. It'd been a while since he last saw him, and Benji was quick to notice his height. He had a few inches on Mayor Perkins now, and was mighty proud of it. Tobias took every opportunity to stand next to his father, and when he did, he'd extend his spine and raise his chin to amplify the difference.

Out of the four siblings, Benji wouldn't be surprised if Tobias took the next spot as mayor of Wishville. The siblings were practically bound to run against each other, not that anyone else in town was forbidden from running. It was common understanding that a Perkins had always been mayor, and that was just another piece of Wishville not willing to change.

Mrs. Perkins and the mayor sat, their backs and necks in straight alignment, as though preparing to sing.

The twins fought over who got the prized seat, the one closest to the corner. Benji never understood their obsession for that seat. "I don't wanna have to squeeze out," one said. "I call corner."

When the decision was settled, everyone was seated except for Sam. They waited awhile, the food steaming from the platters to the ceiling. Benji watched the steam rise, his mouth watering. Yet simultaneously, he also wanted Sam to take her time.

Benji waited for them to call Sam into the room, but Mrs. Perkins was far too gentle for that. She slipped out of her seat and hovered down the hallway, her dress rippling beautifully behind her. When she returned, her arm was wrapped around Sam. She guided her into the last set seat—the one across from Benji. Neither of them looked at each other.

The moment Mrs. Perkins' sat, the twins attacked the food, competing over who could fit the most on their plates.

When the effects of the war had settled, Benji reached

for his own helping. Seeing that Sam had her arms crossed, the adults plated themselves next over chitchat.

"Can you believe these two will be high schoolers soon?" Mrs. Perkins asked. "They grow up so fast."

Rebecca smiled. "They do."

Tobias tapped Benji gently on the head with a flat palm. "Most of them do, at least." He took a bite of bread, the twins laughing hysterically in the background. Benji smiled away the joke, but Mrs. Perkins must have sensed him uncomfortable. She scolded Tobias with a voice soft enough to be a compliment. "Please don't tease."

Sam wasn't amused. She leaned back in the chair, her arms crossed and her hair as frizzy as ever. It looked as if she'd been sleeping the whole day. Benji didn't judge her, though. So had he.

Normally meals were busy. Three conversations would go on at once. One between the brothers, one between Rebecca and the adults, and the last between Sam and Benji. Perhaps all three had to be functioning for the others to exist, because the room stood silent. Their eyes followed him throughout the meal. All of them except Sam's, at least.

"Is something wrong?" Mayor Perkins asked.

It took awhile for Benji to realize he was talking to him. "Oh, sorry. I'm just thinking about a few things."

"You two seem dense," one of the twins said. The other elbowed Sam in the side, an action she had evidently picked up from them. "Got in a little lovers' quarrel?"

Benji took a long sip of water, trying not to focus on their laughter. He stared at Sam through the glass. She looked as if she were about to explode. Her face grew more and more red until it finally happened. Sam burst.

"He tried to leave."

The room grew silent. Benji nearly spit out his water, not able to believe the words that left her mouth. There were a few secrets acceptable to slide, and this was certainly not one of them. He stared at Sam deep in the eye, but she didn't look at him. Her eyes were on her empty plate.

Mayor Perkins set down his fork. "What do you mean by that?"

"Yeah." Rebecca turned to Benji. "What does she mean by that?"

The twins turned to each other in confusion, and Tobias scratched his head. "Tried to leave what?"

Benji waited. He stared at Sam, waiting for her to cover it. He waited for her to say *leave school before the test* and then whisper *karma* into his ears later in the evening. He wanted it to be some kind of payback for whatever he did that had bothered her so much the day before. But she said none of that. Instead, she faced him and stared right through his soul. "Benji tried to leave Wishville."

That was the end of it. Benji had pictured the scenario several times in his mind. What would happen if word got loose of what he had tried to do? What would people think of him? How would people react? And the fact that the Mayor, his father's best friend, of all people, was sitting at the table hearing the words for himself was anything but good.

The attention shifted. There was no more confusion about Sam. No more stares in her direction. Instead, everyone turned to Benji, and the room went cold. The meal on his plate was suddenly unappetizing.

"Benji," Mayor Perkins said, "is this true?"

CHAPTER 11

red

"Let me get this straight." Rebecca collapsed onto the couch, her face burrowing deep into her palms. "You tried to leave because you *needed* to know what was out there?"

He faced the rug.

"Benji."

"Yes." He nodded. "Yes, that's what I just explained."

The room was cold.

When the moment passed, Rebecca hunched over and took a deep breath. "Please, sit down," she said. "I want you to explain everything. From the beginning."

"I did." Benji stood firm. "I already told you everything."

Rebecca sat on the sofa for a while, her face slowly growing more red by the moment. Without alarm she stormed from her sitting position and raised her chin to look at her son right in the eye. "Sit."

And this time, Benji sat.

His mom clutched at the fabric of her cardigan. "I want to believe you." She paced across the room. "I do.

But you've been so secretive lately. You never told me you almost left Wishville. Sam did it for you."

Benji's eyes didn't lift off the ground. He pulled his arms close to his stomach and wiggled his toes in the carpet. The room darkened by the second. He couldn't tell if the sun was setting, or if Rebecca's shadow was standing in the way. The weight of the air around him was dense, leaving his shoulders sore from the pressure. If he said nothing, Rebecca would be even more furious.

Maybe I should try explaining myself.

"You'll listen to me?"

Even though he didn't look at her, something about the room told him she had softened. The walls lightened, and she sat on the opposite end of the couch. "I'm always listening."

So he told her. He told her everything starting with the time Nina first acted strange toward him—May 4th. He told her about how she predicted her death the night before. He told her about how everyone had fallen apart. He explained everything.

When Benji was toward the end of his story, Rebecca shook her head. "Wow."

Benji's arms relaxed. "The day she told me about her death, she also gave me this red—"

"I can't believe this." Rebecca's pupils were like yo-yos, twirling as she tried to gather her thoughts. "I can't believe you'd come up with such an elaborate story to cover up some stupid mistake."

Benji's forehead was riddled with folds. "Mom?"

"Go to your room." Rebecca pointed toward the hall. "I don't want to see you until you decide to tell me the truth."

Benji stood from the couch. "I told you everything!"

"Well *I* told you to go to your room!" She was red now, breathing like a bull.

It was one person. One person was all it took for Benji to feel as if all of Wishville were against him. It wasn't like this with Sam, Chloe, or even with James. This was worse than disappointment. It was tangier and more pungent. The smell of betrayal.

He slammed his bedroom door behind him, shut off the lights, then slammed a fist against the wall. "Stupid." He turned to the ground, clenching his eyes shut. "Stupid, stupid."

The only source of light in his room was the dim glow of the moon from his window. As Benji leaned against the door, his teeth clenched, arm pulsing, his eyes shot over to a hint of red.

A beautiful envelope sitting on his desk.

Benji shut his eyes until all he saw were the shapes and colors of his brain. After a few seconds, his mind turned white. They opened once more, and the envelope was still in his hands. It wasn't a nightmare set to disappear.

"I can't do it." Benji lifted the envelope in front of him, ready to blast it across the room. "I can't!" But instead of letting go, his grip on the paper intensified until he could nearly feel the words through the paper.

What would happen if I knew how it all ends?
What if I opened the envelope?
What if I discovered the truth?

I could plan my future.

I could—

Benji blinked, and the thoughts disappeared. "Should I do it?" He searched the room, waiting for a response. When the moonlight quivered and the silence stood firm, he lowered his eyes back to the future in his grasp.

The envelope didn't open willingly. It took him a while. At each attempt the paper would rip at an angle, creating a strange tab-like fling of rips off the side of the envelope. He paused, waiting for himself to change his mind, but it didn't.

The envelope was finally torn across, wide enough for him to retrieve the paper from inside. It appeared to be a page ripped from a notebook. Folded in half, it mocked him, as if to say, *This is your last chance. You don't have to do it.*

Benji's hand shook as he brought it closer to his face. With the sight of pencil marks through the thin paper, he pulled his swollen eyes away and locked them to the wall. Without looking, he parted the paper with his tangled fingers and held the finished product tight enough to choke the writing off the page. He was about to read.

"Don't do it." There was no one there to stop him. The words had come from his own mouth. He slammed his lips shut and breathed in short intervals.

"Don't do it." He leaned over, a sharp pain overrunning his stomach. "Don't do it, Benji."

But no matter what he said, the paper would not let him be. It stood proudly in his fingertips. He waited for it to crawl back into the tattered envelope where it belonged, but it refused to even look in that direction.

He bit his quivering lip and forced his eyes from the

wall to the opened paper. He read the date. He saw it with his own two eyes.

Benji leaned in closer. The date didn't change.

He pushed the paper further away. No difference.

The page fluttered to the ground and Benji scooted away, as if it were infested with some kind of disease. The idea of shutting his eyes made him shiver. The paper was like a spider on the wall. He didn't want to take his eyes off of it with fear the beast might disappear.

Benji collapsed to the floor, refusing to breathe. "No."

He stood there for a while, his focus locked on the paper resting in front of him. The town spun, but by the time he calmed his dizziness and lifted his head, his mind was blank. All that was left was a date imprinted in his brain, echoing through him in burning waves.

A date that would greet him seven days away.

Part II

wishville

CHAPTER 12

stricket

The forbidden hill. Benji wasn't sure what brought him here.

Three hours ago the red envelope lay at his side, opened. The paper in his hands, read. There was nothing to do. No way to escape. He chose to stare death in the eye, and because of this choice, he could no longer look away.

Dew shimmered on the grass clearing, lighting the way to a lonely house nested on Eudora Hill. It was where Oliver Stricket lived, and therefore was a place no one dared to visit. A desolate house, yet it called across town and lured him here.

It was nearly three in the morning. The realization that he was on Eudora Hill froze him, and his last bits of reason urged him to return home. To crawl back in bed and end this. End all of this craziness. Convince himself the color red was a lie. But he knew he wouldn't be able to sleep no matter how convincingly he recreated the truth. He knew he'd go mad anyway.

Some called Oliver dangerous. A few used the word

psycho. At this point, why should that matter? Benji wouldn't die tonight, anyway, so what was the harm?

The grass was untouched, not the slightest bend of a strange. His sneakers smashed the grass into patches as he crossed the clearing. "Sorry."

Great, now I'm talking to plants.

The moonlight washed over him, lighting the grass in a vivid array of greens. Shadows of the surrounding trees amplified the hill's brightness with their striking contrast. Crackling of crickets filled the air from all directions. A moth glided past his ear, and Benji watched its wings disappear among the stars, revealing a radiant full moon.

The moss-covered deck of Oliver's house shivered under his feet. He paused, waited for the deck to settle, and knocked on the door. Three bold, heavy knocks.

Before he could pull his arm away, the windows of the house lit with golden light and the door burst open, barely missing his nose.

A man appeared in the doorway. His eyes, although blazing with a fiery alertness, drooped over his cheeks, and he reached to rub them.

"What do you want?" Oliver's voice reminded Benji of the ocean. Frantic, yet smooth. Violent, yet delicate.

Benji had nothing to say. He wasn't sure what he wanted, or even why he came. The chilling air draped over him in a blanket, and he rubbed his bare arms. He left home without a jacket.

"Look, you need to leave." He tightened his grip on the doorknob, but something stopped him from shutting it.

"Hey, kid. Stop crying."

Benji couldn't.

Oliver searched the clearing before stepping aside, allowing Benji to enter.

Benji stepped into the house and wiped his face dry.

The inside was tidier than he'd imagined. The furniture was minimal, but each piece served its purpose. Books stacked against the walls so high they nearly covered all the beige paint. Oliver flicked another light on, illuminating a television on the far end of the room. The last time Benji had seen one was in the school library, and he couldn't remember the last time he'd been there.

"You like the TV?" Oliver approached the old device. "Not many of them in town. Even if you've got one the only thing on it's the Wishville News Channel. They loop it all day." He clicked a button on the side, lighting the screen with a quick static flash of green.

"—to a shocking discovery. This month is expected to receive the most rain Wishville has seen in decades, along with a slight chance of flooding." It was the same voice Benji heard echo through the house every morning as Rebecca ate breakfast with a dose of news. Must've been the same as the radio broadcast, but with some added visuals.

Oliver shut the TV off, waiting for Benji to speak. He tried, he really did, but he couldn't get the words to flow. Instead, he stared at Oliver's cracked lips and uncombed hair.

"Sorry." Benji backed into the hall. "I should go."

As he reached for the doorknob, Oliver cleared his throat. "You're Scott's kid, aren't you?"

"How did you—"

"Just a hunch." There was hint of safety in his muddy eyes. "I'll get you some water."

He disappeared into another room, the door hinges squealing like wild boars. Benji skeptically trailed along the edges of the living room, observing every detail, searching for something off. This was his chance to leave. His chance to go where he knew he'd be safe. At least, where he'd be safe for a week. Or maybe something bad would happen before that. Maybe home wasn't safe at all. Maybe—

"Here." Oliver thrust a mug into Benji's hand. "Chug it. You'll feel better."

Benji watched the liquid whirl in his hand as he raised the mug to his lips. The chilled water spilled into the void of his empty stomach, and he felt a pinch more like himself.

"Benji Marino, right?" Oliver took the mug from him and set it on a nearby stack of books.

"Why do you—"

"No one's been here in years." Oliver crossed his arms. "What happened to you?"

"I think . . ." Benji's arms went stiff. "I think I'm dying."

"You're sick?"

"No."

"Is someone after you?"

"No!"

The man shut his mouth, waiting.

"If I tell you what happened," Benji said, "you'll think I'm crazy."

Oliver grinned, and for a brief moment, his eyes lifted. "Well, that'd make two of us."

Benji tried to conjure the memories, but they were difficult to recall. The events were so disastrous that they crashed into each other, forming a blur in his mind, but with some concentration, he understood where the story began.

Benji gulped. "You've heard of Nina Koi?"

His eyes widened. "Walter and Cheryl had a second kid?"

Humor struck Benji for a brief second, dissipating before he could smile. "She passed away less than a week ago."

Oliver nodded, urging him to go on.

"She told me exactly when she'd die, and she was right. But before that, she gave me an envelope. Said it contained the date and time of my death."

"And you opened it?"

Benji bit his lip to keep the tears from forming again.

"Jeez kid, you've got guts!"

"I have seven days left."

Oliver sat on the couch, motioning for Benji to join him. "May 23rd?"

"Yeah, at night."

"She give you a time?"

"11:59."

Oliver folded his hands in front of his face, pressing his nose against his thumbs. "I see."

"You mean you believe me?"

"It's not that I believe you." His voice was muffled from his hands. "I simply believe it'd be ignorant of me to think I know everything about this world. And if you trust this girl enough to come here, of all places, then perhaps there's truth to what you say."

Oliver cleared his throat. He waited for the man to speak, but he never did, so Benji continued. "I opened it after an argument with a friend. She was mad at me, and she told a secret that turned my mom against me. I was frustrated and—"

"Until you accept that life will go on without you, you might as well be living this week dead. That's something I've learned up here." He set his arms down. "What's something you've always wanted to do?"

Benji ran his fingers through his wavy hair. "Leave Wishville."

"And what's stopping you?"

"My friends always get in the way. And when I come back from the bridge, it's like I'm stuck here."

"That's a lie. You're standing in the way of yourself."

Benji could have left during the night, without any written plans. No one would've predicted it. If he wanted to, he could've left tonight, but he didn't. Despite how much time he had left, he stayed.

Maybe Oliver was right.

"You're not letting yourself leave because you know you aren't ready yet."

He pictured his failed escape. He practically gave up after one try. Every day, every hour, every minute since then was a missed opportunity to leave.

"No one wants to be forgotten. You're attached to Wishville because you don't have a legacy to leave behind. So let me ask you again. What's something you've always wanted to do?"

Benji didn't have to think. "I've always wanted to do something different. To bring some color to this place."

"Accomplish that, and passing the bridge should be a piece of cake."

"And then what?"

"You'll be ready for anything that comes."

"You mean, I'll be ready to die?"

Oliver chuckled. "Look, I'm not some kind of all-knowing being. But I do think that your purpose is to bring some change to this devil of a town."

"All of that? Change Wishville, leave town?" Benji tapped his foot against the floor. "Mr. Stricket, I only have seven days."

"I hate Stricket. Call me Oliver. Now tell me, Benji. Is this really what you want?"

"What?"

"Are you sure you want to leave?"

Benji nodded.

"Say it."

"I want to leave."

"This is *your* choice, okay?" A storm struck the ocean of his voice. It was rapid, unpredictable, defensive. "If you leave, I have nothing to do with it."

"How about you?" Benji frowned. "Are you ready to die?"

Oliver leaned into the couch. "Well, there is this one regret I'd like to resolve first. But it's not important." His shoulders were tense. "This is about you."

They sat in silence on the highest-standing building in town. Together on the forbidden hill. Benji couldn't understand how everyone saw Oliver as crazy. He wasn't normal, but he was kind. And kindness wasn't a valid reason to make him an outcast.

"I should go." Benji stood. "Oliver?"

"Yes?"

"Could I come back tomorrow?"

"You're always welcome here." He didn't stand. "But whatever you do, don't tell anyone about your visits."

CHAPTER 13

grass

James tuned out the haunting chatters of the hallway as he entered his combination. Inside his locker was an organized arrangement of textbooks, sorted by the order of his classes, and a stack of books on the second shelf, stacked from least enjoyable to his second-favorite. He spun his books around so the spines no longer faced him, the sight of their familiar titles nauseating.

Chloe appeared next to him with a glass container in the cup of her hands. "Aw darn, you beat me." She reached inside the glass and pulled out a cookie. "Thought I was always the extra-early one."

James nodded, a vague sign of acknowledgment. He pulled out his English textbook from the far left side of his locker and slid it into his empty backpack. By the time he shut his locker, Chloe had already moved onto her second cookie.

"What are you staring at?" She chuckled, cookie crumbs smeared across her chin, chocolate chips blended around her mouth like dark lipstick. "You want one?"

James retrieved a cookie from the glass. It was warm. "Whoa, there. I was kidding." She stepped away, playfully shielding the remaining cookies with her open arm. "Since when do you eat sweets?"

His jaw tensed as he sunk his teeth through it.

"So, what do you think?"

"Dry."

Sam joined them in their hallway gathering. He could tell something was brewing in her mind by the way she picked at the callouses on her fingers and hummed a solo violin piece as Chloe spoke proudly of her over-baked cookies.

"Probably my best work." Chloe shut the container with a snap of the lid. "Sam, you good?"

She stopped humming. "What?"

"You dying or something?"

Sam threw her back against the lockers and glued it there. "Just tired." There was no explanation. No rant. Sam's two-word statement must have been the record for her shortest complaint.

While Sam lurked in her own mind, Chloe trying to coax her out of it, James ate the last bite of his brick cookie.

Normally Benji would show up right before the bell rang, pushing time to its limits. He was the type to walk slower if he was on track to arrive five minutes early. He enjoyed seeing how close he could come to being late without actually being marked tardy. James assumed he did it for the thrill. Something to quench that everyday thirst for adventure that would otherwise devour him from the inside.

But today, Benji walked passed them with a familiar spark in his eyes. The kind of spark James saw him wearing on the bridge that day.

It was 7:34. 26 minutes before class. Some kids were already at school for morning club meetings, socializing, studying for a first-period test, or with an intense fear of showing up late. But Benji? Coming this early was unheard of.

He rushed by, hands tucked in his sweatshirt pocket. His focus glazed right over them.

"Benji!" Chloe called.

He stopped, and the stiffness of his arms gave James the impression he knew they stood there all along.

"I made these last night." She lifted the glass container. "Come try one."

Benji looked at James, his smile softening before turning away. "Sorry," he said. "I don't have much time. I'm sure they're great, though."

"You're early." Chloe ran her hand down her braided hair. "What do you mean you don't have time?"

Benji was trapped in the hallway sea. Students washed around his sides, joking about Coach Hendrick's new green whistle, complaining about the morning fog. He was disconnected from his friends, but he made no effort to step closer and penetrate the water that divided them. "I'll see you guys later." As he merged with the flow of middle school traffic, Sam banged her fist against the lockers.

"That kid." She pulled her hand away, shaking it with a wince. "Thinks it's all about him."

Before Chloe could say anything, Sam pushed off into the sea Benji had disappeared in only moments ago. As James watched the two of them move away, his blood simmered. The isolation was warm, comforting, and he wanted to go there too.

Chloe undid her braid. "I feel like I missed something." She combed her fingers through her hair to loosen the unnatural coils. "Are they still mad about lunch yesterday?"

James remembered all the lunches they shared together. How many hours was it combined? How much time did he waste wandering the halls, chatting with three kids who he shared nothing in common with? He watched the ocean through the hallway window. The waves twisted in unison with the movement of students in the hall, and he joined them, submersing himself.

One, two, three . . .

Chloe called after him, but he didn't hear. The only noise that filled him as he walked alone to class was the roaring of numbers in his head.

Nine, eight, seven . . .

James and Sam sat alone at their desks before the bell rang, distracting themselves to the point that they didn't notice each other. James pulled out his book after a few moments, simply by habit, but managed to stop himself before opening it. His fingers tightened around the cover of *Sharpner's Peak*.

Two, three, four . . .

He set the book down.

His classmates trickled into the room, but his counting was too loud for him to notice. By the time Chloe walked in, his mind was in another world.

As usual, Benji arrived seconds before the first bell rang. James stopped counting when he realized that Benji had come to school early, but not to class. Benji slipped into his seat, sweating, holding his heavy breaths in an effort not to draw attention to himself. To most, his appearance was normal, unnoticed, but when James looked closer, he saw grass splattered across Benji's socks like paint.

CHAPTER 14

calendar

Benji's desk drawers were crammed with useless junk. Old exam scores. Some candy wrappers. A school calendar.

Wait, a calendar. That could work.

He lifted it from the drawer of rubbish like rescuing a drowning child from the water. Each student had received one on the first day of school. He never used them, no one did, but this week would be an exception.

Benji sat at his desk with a red pen. He flipped to the May page and inhaled the dusty air.

Wrapping his cold fingers around the pen, he brought it closer to the 23rd day. In two heavy strokes, he drew a large X through the pristine, empty square. Such a random day. He knew no one with a birthday on the 23rd. Not one holiday on that date. Yet here he was, witnessing such a random day become the most important one in his life.

"Six days left." He folded the earlier month pages over the spine before slipping the calendar into an empty drawer of his desk. "I won't die in this town."

He unpacked his backpack, shoving his homework

into the top drawer of his dresser, which he had designated to be his homework drawer. All of his work from the past week was sitting there waiting for him. He had placed them inside with the intent of eventually catching up, but now that the clock was ticking, was there even a point? He added today's assignments onto the heap of papers and shut it. His back muscles loosened.

The sketchbook on top of his desk caught his attention. He turned a few pages, observing the colorful landscapes and buildings. One by one, he flipped through, soaking in the details, until all that greeted him were white pages. After shutting his sketchbook, he tossed it into the drawer along with his worthless homework assignments.

The final task on his list for today was to make dinner. By the time Rebecca got home there was a cold platter of fish on the table, and a side of salad and green beans straight from the can. Nothing extravagant, but it was the best he could do. Rebecca stared at Benji, and he stared back, pulling the widest grin he could handle.

"What's all this?"

"Thought I'd make dinner." Benji slid two plates onto the table before plopping into his usual seat. "And I wanted to apologize. About trying to leave and all."

Rebecca nodded as she sat. "Actually, I think I might've been harsh on you as well. I was—you know—worried I might lose you, too. You're what keeps me living." She plated her meal and took a few bites of undercooked fish. "I'm really shocked you did all this. You've never been the type to apologize first. I don't remember you being so mature."

"I guess I'm just getting older."

When Rebecca had finished her plate, she set down her fork and sighed. "I'll accept what you tried to do, but you need to promise me that you'll never do it again." She shook her head. "Okay? I don't even want you *thinking* about getting near that bridge. Not even—"

"Don't worry, Mom." Benji smiled, and it hurt. "I promise."

CHAPTER 15

audrey

"Um . . . hi?" Lauren faced him at the door. Her hair was a tangled mess, and she was still dressed in her pajamas. Benji knew it was odd for him to randomly show up at her home. He hadn't been to Lauren's place since she first moved out of her parents' house and Rebecca brought her a bag of cookies to celebrate.

"Can I ask for a favor?"

"It better be important, shortie." Lauren stepped aside. "I don't like waking up for no reason."

Benji trailed after her. "I woke you?"

"What, you think I'm an early riser?" Lauren laughed as she shut the door behind them.

Her house was exactly how he remembered it. Light seeped through the many curtainless windows, giving the bamboo floors a dewy glow. The only piece of decoration she had in the room was a single cactus plant displayed at the center of her oak dining table. Lauren had always been a simple person. She never cared for unnecessary furniture, unless coffee and espresso machines counted. She had five of those lined up against the kitchen counter. Benji assumed it was more for aesthetics than functionality. She would've been fine without one, considering she spent most of her daylight hours at Seaside Cafe.

"Benji?"

"Huh?"

"The favor."

"Oh, right!" Benji reached for his head, running a hand through his hair. "I wanna get rid of it."

Lauren leaned against the kitchen island. "Get rid of what?"

"My hair."

"Um . . ." Lauren frowned. "You want me to shave your head?"

Benji's eyes widened. "No. Oh, gosh no. Just cut it."

"*Cut* your head?"

"My hair."

Lauren smiled in disbelief. "Benji, you've had that same haircut since you were little."

"So?"

"Why would you wanna change it all of a sudden? It's cute."

"No, it's not cute. It's annoying." Benji flicked his hair so it fell over his face, covering his eyes. "If it's like this I can't see."

"Easy. Don't push it in your eyes like that."

He pushed his hair aside, and their eyes met. Tension grew until Lauren finally snapped.

She sighed. "Okay."

"Really?"

She nodded. "But Rebecca knows about this, right?"

Benji narrowed his eyes. "Does she *own* my hair?"

"Good point." She headed toward the hallway. "I'll

do it, but I'm getting changed first. Eat some cereal or something. You know where it is."

"You know I don't eat breakfast."

"Well you do in this house."

The hallway was filled with eyes. Eyes of all kinds of colors and shapes—completely different from each other in every way—yet all drawn to the same subject. Benji was too lost in his own world to care, and the eyes were too shy to step into such an unfamiliar land. They backed aside.

A fear infected the students of Wishville Junior High. Benji's haircut was frightening. Drew eyes to him only to scare the eyes away. This unfamiliar world Benji was in—the place his eyes were lost in—something about it made the students uneasy.

Sam couldn't watch. She stared at her sneakers and hummed a new song, and Benji, recognizing it, hummed along as he staggered down the hall. Chloe came toward him, smiling at first, but when Benji noticed her, stepped aside as though she had seen a stranger for the first time. Benji progressed down hall. He he saw James shut his locker and disappear toward the classroom door, not a single glance in his direction.

"Is that you, Marino?" Jett blocked Benji's way in the hall, hands in his pockets and slouching with a spine made of goop. The fear didn't faze him. "Gosh, you turn into more of a freak each day."

Benji stopped, Jett proving not to move out of the way. "Well," Benji said, "you're not wrong."

The hallway children shifted through him. Benji was a ghost. They saw him and were frightened, so they now moved past him, trying to convince themselves that he wasn't real, that he couldn't exist, that what they saw was fake.

"You cut your hair." There it was. Jett said it.

Benji nodded. "I did."

"You cut it . . . weird."

"You think?" Benji ran a hand through his short hair, his face calm. "Thanks, thought I'd go for something new."

Jett narrowed his eyes at Benji, and Benji smiled back. Two silver moons rested on his starry cheeks. He didn't care what Jett said, didn't bother being annoyed by him. Jett was another classmate, another person he'd miss after being gone. Yeah, he'd miss him. He'd miss the class clown, the failing bully, the insensitive jerk that the school tried to deny their love for. He made class slightly more interesting. Brought a few more colors to the dull school they lived in.

"What the hell's gotten into you?" Jett's neck was tense, his brows were twisted, and his eyes searched through the blankness. That's when the fear came. That's when he felt it, when it hit him like it did the rest of the hall. He took a step back, gripping the straps of his backpack as a lifeline.

By the time lunch rolled around, the fear had faded. It faded in the same way it did when Benji came early for the first time, when his classmates saw him with grass on his socks and two new friends. The fear, the shock, the confusion, it faded with a meager dose of time.

Benji left Mr. Trenton's class to find Alex and Ray waiting at the door. They were seventh-graders on the school soccer team, about the same height, and looked similar, although not a speck related. Nearly identical shades of dusty blond hair, matching basketball shorts, and a freckle on each of their left cheeks. A resemblance striking enough to notice, but not worth mentioning.

Ray threw a soccer ball at Benji, and he caught it.

Alex and Ray's eyes widened in unison, but when the shock dissipated, they laughed.

"You're crazy." That was Ray, the one wearing the bold blue shirt Benji hadn't noticed before. The colors seeped into his brain, and when Benji turned to Alex, who was now twisting the length of his own hair, all he focused on was his orange and green striped polo.

"Almost makes me wanna do the same," Alex said. "*Almost.*"

Benji tossed the soccer ball gently between his hands, watching the black pentagons spin in hypnotizing patterns. He'd been wishing to join the soccer team for years. Sure, he hadn't done it. Rebecca would never allow him to. But she never said he couldn't toss a soccer ball around with a couple of seventh-graders in his free time.

Unlike how Benji pictured himself playing soccer, he had absolutely no coordination. He not only struggled with foot tricks, but simple dynamics too, like judging what strength and angle to kick the ball at for it to reach someone else. Either he lacked natural talent or these seventh-graders had supernatural abilities. They could do anything they wanted with their feet. They were free. Meanwhile, Benji had gotten to school extra early this morning to learn how to pop the ball into the air and catch it. He was unsuccessful.

Alex and Ray had always known Benji, but not well. They'd gone to the same school for the majority of their educational lives, being only a year apart, and yet they hardly spoke to each other. Benji remembered giving Alex advice on how to do well on Mr. Miller's pop quizzes back in fifth grade. He once asked Ray when soccer season started, although he didn't remember when or why he asked. So the idea of surprising these two kids had thrilled him.

At first the two had been skeptical. Eighth-grade Benji Marino? The boy who never joined a sport? The boy with the overprotective mom, who showed up almost late to every class, who lost his dad ten years ago? What was Benji Marino doing at school early, standing in the field, asking for them to teach him how to play soccer?

He stopped tossing the soccer ball in his hands. There was no time for reminiscing about yesterday. He had work to do.

Audrey stepped out of class, heading toward the music room.

Ray adjusted the collar of his polo. "You're coming, right?"

Alex, somehow sensing Benji had other plans, held out his hands. "Stop by if you have time."

"Sure thing." Benji tossed the soccer ball into Alex's arms, his focus locked on Audrey. As soon as the two boys left, he rushed after her.

"Hey." Benji reached Audrey's side. "Can we talk?"

She stopped in the middle of the hall, so he did, too. Her eyes traced Benji's hair. "It looks nice." There was a hint of skepticism in her voice, but Benji didn't acknowledge it. "Is everything okay?"

"Oh, yeah. Yeah, I'm fine." Benji crossed his arms to relax them. "There's been a lot on my mind lately. I've actually been meaning to tell you something for a while."

"Okay?"

"I like you." His arms stiffened again, and he bit his lip to keep from walking away.

Audrey was a sculpture. Her black hair rested over her shoulders as if they had been melted onto her, motionless. When she finally moved, it was only to face the ground.

Benji couldn't handle the silence anymore, so he continued. "Since fourth grade, actually."

"I see." That was all she said.

Five years. He had spent the last five years waiting for Audrey's smile. The smile that lit the classroom, filled it with colors he could hardly imagine. There was no denying the fact that she was beautiful. Everyone could see that. But had he really known her?

Five years. Five years of intoxication, that's what it was. He wasn't thinking of Audrey when he tried to leave earlier this month. He wasn't thinking of her when he imagined his future. She brought a dash of color to a town as desaturated as Wishville, and Benji clung to all the colors he knew to survive. Every speck of it he gripped with his soul. But now that he had finally said it, now that the words came loose, these bottled feelings washed away.

The truth was, he never liked Audrey.

He liked the colors she showed. The colors gave him hope that someday, life could change. She was a distraction from searching for the truth, searching for the true colors, the permanent ones.

"I liked you, Audrey." Their eyes met. "But I felt like I should still tell you."

"Well, thanks." When she smiled this time, the colors were gone. "For telling me."

Benji smiled back, and his arms relaxed at his sides. He was lighter. Weightless.

Floating.

CHAPTER 16

pages

His last day at Blueberry.

James sat cross-legged on the rug, *Sharpner's Peak* in hand. He wasn't particularly sure what had brought him to the old shed. It wasn't the silence. Wasn't the nostalgic buzz of his childhood second-home. It was unidentifiable, but necessary.

Today was Blueberry's funeral. He would pay one final visit. Think back on bittersweet memories. Pay his respects. And when he finished, the place would be erased from his life forever, only a memory associated with the most beautiful and morbid part of his life.

He stared at the rotting door, the rusty storage shelf where they stashed their secret junk food, the black specks sprinkled across the ceiling like stars in the sky, accumulating in the corners. He ran his hand along the dusty carpet beneath him, smelled the salty air of the nearby ocean, tasted blood from the cheek he realized he'd been biting.

He thought back on the time he spent with his friends. Benji, Chloe, Sam, all three of them pulling him into their silly games. They convinced him to waste his time.

Accepted him with all of his faults. They embraced his love of books and puzzles and everything that destroyed his integrity, and in doing so, didn't give him a reason to change.

All the time he buried himself inside of Blueberry with three kids who had the time to waste. They were stuffed with it, boundless loads of it, almost too much of it to bear. And yet there he was, tagging along the eternal children while his own sister's clock ticked with threatening alarm.

He stood, leaving his book abandoned on the rug, and leaned against the wall. With a clear view of the room, the memories appeared clearly in front of him. Sam ranted about something while Benji tuned her out. Chloe walked in behind them and shut the door. She looked at James.

How many times had he been here in this room, wasting his life away while his sister fought to keep hers?

"Didn't think you'd be here." Chloe kicked a floorboard, Benji and Sam vanishing.

"You're real," James said.

"Yep, alive and breathing." She inhaled a gust of wind into her mouth and coughed. "At least, I hope so. Why'd you come here, anyway?"

He tapped his head.

"Me too. Just wanted a chance to think someplace new. The house gets old sometimes." She jumped to the door. "Let's go on a walk."

James unglued his back from the wall, but his feet didn't budge.

"Oh, come on." She walked down the steps, her

voice echoing behind her. "It's not like we don't have time to kill."

James grabbed his book and followed her through the forest. The crunching of twigs under their feet diminished as they reached the ocean, meeting a floor that flashed between blue, white, and gray.

The shore on this side of Wishville was not only rockier than the other, but also layered with fallen pine needles. Chloe took her shoes off anyway.

James planted his feet and shook his head, establishing his stance on the matter.

"What a nerd." She rolled off her socks into wads, tossed them onto the prickly sand, and jumped toward the shore, giggling as the rocks poked into her feet. She leaned over to roll her leggings up, and James cleared his throat.

"Calm down, I'm not planning to go in." She straightened her back and stepped forward.

"You could drown."

"I said, I'm not planning to go." She kicked at the sand, watching the splashes ripple through the waves. "Have Benji and Sam been acting weird to you lately?"

James tapped his foot unsuccessfully. His shoes sunk into the ground.

"Benji has to be up to something. I heard he's been coming to school early to play soccer with Alex and Ray. Then Peyton told me about Audrey today. I've been trying to get him to tell her for years, and he does it out of nowhere?" The waves reached for her toes, but she stepped back before they could touch her. "Then there's Sam. She's been distracting herself with all that boring music stuff, I can tell. Either I'm missing something or there's maggots in my brain."

"Or maybe it's time to move on." A breeze rushed between them, creating a wall of chilling air.

"Are you kidding?" Chloe spun around so fast it was practically a hop. "You guys are my family. I'm not letting this get any worse."

She crossed from damp sand to dry, past James, and threw herself at the ground where she'd placed her shoes. "You'd be fine if we all fell apart?" She pulled her socks back over her muddy feet and slipped her boots on. "We've been friends forever."

James glanced at the book in his hands. It's bloody red cover.

Chloe stood. "Moving on is different from pushing people away."

When he raised his chin, Chloe was still for once. Not jumping around or fidgeting with her hair. Her feet were planted to the ground, her arms crossed, and her hair lying flat against her face, held still by the surrounding trees which blocked the windy air. All that moved were her eyes, quivering as they searched James's face for recognition. "Maybe you really do need some time to yourself." After a slow blink, her eyes stopped shifting.

"Bye, Chloe." He won this battle.

As Chloe retreated into the forest, he stepped toward the shore again, the grip on his favorite book tightening. He couldn't count the amount of hours he had spent forcing his nose deep into the book, watching the world wash away around him. How many hours he had spent next to his sister, but a whole universe away. How many times he must have blocked out those talking to him, prioritizing the dialogue of the novel's more intriguing characters than the mundane ones encountered in his ordinary life. How much time he spent with imaginary people instead of his sister, the sister he knew was dying, but chose to believe would live forever for the sake of his own desires.

The waves squirted mists across his face, and he welcomed them. His fingers gripped to a random page. With a slow, painful drag of his wrist, he ripped it from the spine. The paper dangled between his index finger and thumb, the hazy light making it appear thinner than it really was. He dropped the page, watched it twist and twirl like waves before becoming a part of the real ones, pulled into rotation. James ripped another paper. Dropped it. Another. Dropped.

With each paper he let go, a part of himself deteriorated. He developed a hunger for the ocean to devour every part of himself he hated. Every last word that made him the boy he despised. Soon he was ripping in clumps. His arm was sore, his fingers beaten with paper cuts, but he kept tearing.

The pages of his prized book were gone. All that was left was an unrecognizable book cover with a dented corner. He ran his hands along the cover one last time, ripped it in half by the spine, and chucked it into the water as if tossing bread at seagulls. He watched a piece of the cover float across a peaceful patch before the water drew it into discourse. The cover tossed around, trying to stay afloat, trying to breathe, but was eventually drowned by the current, carried away forever.

Something inside him had shifted. Changed, even. And he couldn't have been more pleased.

CHAPTER 17

cereal

The day had been great. Benji's strange encounter with Audrey had supposedly sparked some color in Wishville Junior High. A few kids even ran into the field at lunch to compliment his hair. But although his plan was progressing seamlessly, the sensation of satisfaction was lacking, replaced by worry as reality seeped in. Benji had been sitting in a tub, a tub filled with the cold-hard fact that his death day was soon to greet him. The news didn't hit him at first. But now, the 23rd was only five days away, and according to his plan, tomorrow would be his last day at school.

Benji had spent too long at Eudora after school. He told Oliver about everything he'd done so far. He lost track of time, barely managing to arrive home before Rebecca returned from work, thanks to his effort to run instead of walk. He rushed to his room, threw his legs under the bed sheets, and shut his eyes. Some would argue it would be wise to never sleep again until his final moment, but what good would that be? More time to do what, exactly? Worry?

The sun shined at his face through open blinds. His

eyes locked shut like the door to a prison cell, blocking all sense of light.

At exactly 3:46 in the afternoon, he fell into a dream.

Benji stood on the bridge. The waves rushed below, threatening him. The tree branches shook rhythmically, calling him. The wind pressed against his back, encouraging him. Past this bridge was a world no one knew.

"What am I doing here?"

His voice was an echo in his brain, fighting to speak, but failing. He could not control his lips, his limbs, or even where to look. The actions took place on their own, and Benji was the observer. He noticed his foot raising, stepping toward the LEAVING WISHVILLE sign. He couldn't restrain himself.

"Stop!" Benji yelled into the sky, but there was nothing to carry the sound. The wind was gone now. So his voice sat there, resonating in his ears. He stepped past the sign. And rather painfully, the other foot jumped and landed ahead of the last.

His heart raced a thousand miles an hour. Although he could see the moon in the foggy sky and hear the icy waves below, he wasn't cold. He was burning, but his sweat evaporated instantly, lifting off into the night sky, stripping him of the last fluids in his body. His tongue was dry.

He turned around, watching Wishville from outside of town.

Benji wasn't sure how, but he could see everything. Chloe arranging her outfit for the following day, Sam practicing the violin, and James lying empty in his bed. Lauren enjoyed her evening coffee, Rebecca flipped through old photographs, and Jett rubbed his forehead as he powered through math homework like a snail.

He could see past Wishville, too. Much further. There were colors in the air he had never seen before, and the mere glance of them broke him from a sweat to a shiver. He turned around to escape the mess, but the colors in this direction were even stronger. Motion were everywhere. Colors were everything.

Benji watched the whole world at once. Everything was moving too fast for him to wrap his mind around, yet tumbling perpetually faster. In almost an instant, Chloe had chosen her outfit, Sam had packed away her violin, James had fallen asleep, and Jett had tossed his incomplete homework into the trash bin.

The world spun beneath his feet. Too fast. "Go back." Time was rushing out of control. "Go back! It's too fast!"

Time did not obey him. He stood frozen, sweating in the middle of the forest, watching the world pivot around him with incredible speed. Every inch of his body ached, and each attempt to move only intensified the soreness. He had been tied with an invisible rope. Couldn't move, couldn't run, couldn't blink. So he stood in pain, watching the world move faster toward the end as if time itself were a bomb.

His mere existence was fading away.

Benji held his shaky hands in front of him. His fingers moved according to his will, and he leaned forward, finding himself back in his room, gripping the bed sheets. He exhaled all of his accumulated worry.

"What happened?" Benji's shoulder burned from Rebecca's tight grip.

He was about to tell her that he was feeling well. That he was fine. But when he opened his mouth, all he knew was that he couldn't breathe.

"Benji." Rebecca shook him. "Did you have a nightmare? Are you okay?"

He caught a single breath. "What—what was I doing?"

"You were shouting in your sleep." Rebecca straightened her back and loosened her grip. "You had me panicked."

Benji leaned to the side, letting Rebecca's hand slip off his shoulder. "I'm going back to sleep." He flopped his head onto his pillow and forced his eyes shut.

"Did something happen? You can tell me, you know."

Benji rolled onto his side, letting sleep take over. It didn't want to, but Rebecca wasn't able to tell. Her soft footsteps tapped against the carpet as she made her way to the door.

The night progressed, but slowly. Every time Benji peeked out the window, the moon was in the same spot as last time. The stars didn't move.

Although Benji reached a point where he didn't think of his death anymore, the bubbling ache in his stomach refused to settle. His forehead was sore to the touch, and when he sat, he realized his nose was runny. He wiped it on his sleeve, sniffled a bit, and rubbed his eyes until they were bone dry.

After a while of staring at the wall, he slipped out of bed and into the hallway.

Benji remembered being younger and walking through the same hallway, afraid something might jump at him. Tonight, there was nothing to be afraid of. he walked with a dull mind, knowing nothing terrible would happen to him. Nothing terrible would happen for five more days, on the night of May 23rd at 11:59.

His shoulder skimmed the wall as he turned the corner. He flicked the kitchen lights on and scavenged the cabinets.

With a sniffle, he lugged a box of chocolate flakes onto the counter with a slam. His head spun, so he paused to balance it before reaching for a bowl.

His stomach rumbled as he opened the refrigerator. He wrapped his cold fingers around the milk handle. His muscles working against him, the jug felt ten times heavier. Perhaps his body was already preparing for death.

He poured a perfect bowl of chocolate flakes. Filled it nearly to the brim. Seeped the milk in halfway. He left the jug and box of cereal on the counter and raised the bowl with shaky white fingers. When he reached the hallway, he turned off the light with his elbow, spilling a few drops of milk on the floor. They shimmered under the illumination of the fridge he had forgotten to shut.

Benji wiped the droplets with his big toe, running the milk into streams across the floor. He frowned, returned to his room, and dropped the bowl onto his desk. The cereal spun inside like a typhoon in the sea. He reached for the spoon.

I forgot a spoon.

He lifted the bowl unsteadily, bringing the edge to his lips. The chocolate flakes seeped into his tongue. When the sensation came that he was about to choke, Benji pulled the bowl away and leaned over his desk, cheeks puffy and filled with cereal. He did his best to chew and swallow, but it refused to go down. Streams of milk trickled from the corners of his lips until there was a perfect amount for him to eat without gagging. He wiped away the sticky milk with his slip.

Any moment now he'd be ready to throw up. He could feel it. In an obscure way, he almost wanted to. It'd be nice to let go of some of the stress clotted inside him. But no matter how much he willed to vomit, all that left him were tears.

They dripped across his cheeks slow enough to wipe away before reaching his chin. At first he could manage to extinguish them, but the more time passed, the faster they came, and he couldn't keep up with them anymore. He wiped repeatedly, but the tears refused to cease. His face was never dry.

So Benji crawled back into bed, silently sobbing into his pillow. A shimmering bowl of soggy cereal waited on his desk.

The voice in his head echoed throughout the night as he clutched the blankets around him. "This is what you wanted, Benji," the voice said. "You asked for change. You asked for something new."

When Benji had calmed the rush of tears and settled his stomach, he peeled away the sheets to see the sun meeting the horizon. Rebecca brushed her teeth in the room next door to the morning weather report chatting through the radio.

He slipped out of bed and changed into the same clothes he wore yesterday. Staring into the mirror with an unfamiliar gaze, he saw the redness in his eyes and the frizziness in his short hair. He rubbed his eyes and ran his fingers through his hair until he was a tad more confident about his image.

Benji smiled.

That same old smile he would smile every day. The smile that proved to everyone in town that he was okay. The smile that perhaps was the only thing about Benji that hadn't changed.

But it didn't feel like he was smiling.

CHAPTER 18

monochrome

Wishville Junior High was foreign to him. The school he'd been in for nearly three years, the school that bored him with its predictable bells, the school that trapped him for seven hours every weekday he was alive—it was bearable, enjoyable. As he walked down the hall, the blooming worries that plagued him throughout the night withered away.

Benji remembered his first day of sixth grade. It was colorful. The evergreen lockers, the glittering ocean waving at him through the hallway window, the rainbow of colors students wore in their unique styles. The colors were everywhere. Vibrant. He was absorbed by them, but soon enough, school grew old, mundane, and he learned to tune the colors out the way a child forgets learning to walk. Wishville Junior High was no longer colorful, but monochrome, only the occasional color appearing to him if he concentrated hard enough, if he really put in the effort. Even then, it was rare.

But on Benji's last day of school, Wishville Junior High was back. He didn't realize the place he'd been introduced to on his first day of sixth grade was missing until it returned.

He saw colors again. The ocean no longer blended into the gray sky. It waved at him. The lockers were as green as the forest. The students wore colors of all shades, even pink and orange, the most subtly obnoxious. He later saw a tinge of red in the sky as he kicked a soccer ball toward Ray in the morning fog.

But what Benji no longer saw were the people who once brought color to his monochrome life. Now they were gray. Fading into the distance, unrecognizable.

He didn't see Chloe lying alone on the rug in Blueberry. Didn't see the picture of the four of them hung in her dining room at the same height as her parents' wedding photo. He didn't see her chasing everyone with glue, trying to piece them back together.

He didn't see the pile of sheet music accumulating on Sam's desk. Didn't see the blisters on her fingers. He didn't see her spending every waking hour practicing the songs, humming them, tapping her fingers against her desk, immersing herself.

He didn't see the books disappearing from James's locker. Didn't see the papers get shredded, burned, soaked, released into the wind. He didn't see the wooden puzzles buried in the backyard of a beautiful home on Main Street.

But at least he saw the colors.

"Please, sit."

Mr. Trenton motioned to a chair facing his desk, and Benji sat.

It was lunch. Benji's last lunch at school, but instead of spending the time how he pleased, Mr. Trenton requested to steal it.

"This doesn't have to be long." The teacher wheeled his chair closer to his desk, tightening the gap between them. "I'd just like to check in."

Benji spotted one of the soccer boys standing outside the classroom window. He was too far for Benji to gauge who he was, considering Alex and Ray's strange similarities. The boy jumped and waved at Benji through the glass, threw a soccer ball into the air, and kicked it down the field.

Mr. Trenton set his elbows on the desk, leaning closer. "Losing someone you care about is one of the most challenging experiences in life. And knowing someone who has to go through loss is often equally challenging."

He peeled his eyes from the window, facing Mr. Trenton's tight grin.

"But I have a feeling this might not be about Nina."

Benji blinked.

Mr. Trenton allowed him the opportunity to speak, but when Benji didn't acknowledge it, slid a single paper toward him. On it was the number *83*.

Benji raised his chin with a smile. "I don't get it."

"This is your English grade exactly one week ago. May 12th. The day you heard the news." He flipped a second page on top. "And this is your grade today."

On it was the number *64* was written boldly in red.

"You haven't been keeping up with the reading, turning in any of your daily assignments, participating in class discussions, and now you're missing two weekly reflections in a row. You also had an essay due today, which I didn't receive. And if that's not enough, Mrs. Crowley told me you turned in a blank paper for your bone-naming test yesterday. She's been reviewing with your class for months." Mr. Trenton raised a fresh pencil from his desk, rubbing his thumb against the unsharpened end. "Look, I know this isn't easy, but there's less than three weeks until the end of the year. If you continue at this rate, you won't be able to graduate."

Three weeks. Only three weeks until he'd be finished with the year and preparing for high school, but he wouldn't make it. He was so close that it left his blood boiling. Today was his last day of school. That was hard enough. But now Mr. Trenton was reminding him of graduation, a day he had looked forward to since the colors disappeared, but would never reach.

"Benji?"

"Sorry. There's been a lot on my mind." He leaned back in his seat, watching Mr. Trenton's forehead in hopes that it'd pass for eye contact.

"Does this have to do with your friends?"

Benji shook his head.

"I hardly see you four together anymore." He spun the pencil around a few more times before tossing it onto the two stacked papers. "If you'd like to talk to me about something—whatever it is—I'm open ears."

Benji relaxed his fist, regaining control. "Sorry about the work. I'll turn everything in next week." The words flew effortlessly off his tongue. Smooth. They were almost sweet.

Mr. Trenton's brows drooped, and his eyes lost that shimmering charm. "Okay." He pursed his lips and nodded his head. "But I hope you keep my words in mind."

"Well," Benji said, "I will admit that I haven't been feeling well lately. I think I might be sick. It's been kinda hard to focus during class."

"I see." His voice was higher than usual, a touch of skepticism. He raised his wrist to check the time. "In that case, you should get some rest. Why don't you head to the office and give your mom a call?"

Friday. May 19th. His final school day as an eighth-grader, and it ended three hours early.

CHAPTER 19

paint

"So, how's it going?"

"Easy." Benji sat on Oliver's living room couch. The house smelled of friendly dust. He had been here only yesterday, yet he missed the place already. Each visit he felt more at home, and slowly, this little hut on Eudora had evolved into his new secret hideout. The *new-and-improved Blueberry.*

"Is that so?" The man stood in front of him, his arms crossed.

He wanted to nod, to tell Oliver that everything was fine, but the tension built until he erupted in a sigh.

"I'm not having the best day." He peeled himself from the backrest of the couch and stared at his sneakers. "I left school early. Was supposed to call my mom first, but I snuck out to the ocean instead."

Oliver wanted to say something, but his jaw shut, and he sat next to Benji. "Why?"

"We graduate on June 6th."

Silence.

"I won't even—I mean—I never had the chance to—"

"You don't have to say it." Oliver set a hand on

Benji's shoulder as he stood. "Wait here. I have something for you."

Benji froze. Each breath was another handful of life taken away. So he held his breath, not that it would help.

He was dealing with a tight pressure building in his throat when something pounded onto the floor in front of him, shocking him into breathing. He leaned forward, squinting at the object.

A bucket of paint.

Oliver set a second bucket down. Gentler this time.

"What's it for?"

"Well . . ." Oliver grinned. "That's up to you. Thought it might spike your creativity."

Benji folded his fingers, waiting for a breakthrough. Nothing came.

"I thought your plan was to bring some change to this place before you left. And I hate to say it, but a little haircut's not enough to put this town through metamorphosis."

The sample color on the lid was a bright green. "Why neon?" Benji asked.

"Cause it's obnoxious."

While Benji thought of an idea for the paint, Oliver sat next to him again. The man's presence was enough for Benji to feel as though all of Wishville was on his side. Finally, he spoke.

"You're a brave kid." Oliver folded his hands on his lap. "But is this really what you want?"

"What do you mean?"

"There's something you should know. You see,

there's a reason why I live on Eudora. A reason why everyone hates me."

Needles filled the air.

"I helped your dad leave."

Benji wasn't as surprised as he expected himself to be. He stood, rubbed his hands over his face, and took a deep breath. "I should go."

"Benji, are you—"

"No, I just need to process this."

"At least hear my side of the story first." Oliver raised his voice. "Benji, sit down."

Hesitantly, he did.

"When I was in high school, I got into fights with Arthur all the time. I didn't believe we could assume leaving town was dangerous without some kind of test. But Arthur, being the know-it-all he was, called me stupid for questioning his belief. At the young age of seventeen he decided that his goal in life was to keep Wishville safe. His emotional public speaking skills made people fear the outside even more. And in place of his overqualified sister, who had other issues she found more important, he became Mayor. What a joke."

Benji shifted in his seat. Oliver sensed he was uncomfortable, because he spoke at a much faster pace. "Of course, it wasn't only Arthur. All kinds of kids laughed at my ideas. Claimed that if I loved the outside so much, I should take a sprint to the other side. Test my own theory."

Benji's body collapsed from his control. He leaned against the back of the couch, face numb, fingers cold.

Oliver continued. "Twenty years passed. I was working at Sequoia Bank on Main Street, finally living a normal life. One day, your dad walked in to withdraw some money. He came to my stand by choice. And as I handed him a fifty-dollar bill, he leaned over and whispered, 'Meet me at Eudora. Tonight at six.'"

"And you went?"

"Of course I did. That night, he apologized to me. Said he had the same questions I did, but never had the heart to ask them. He was scared of what people might think. Scared of losing Arthur as a friend. And after all these years, he was still guilty he never told me I wasn't alone. He promised to make it up to me. That the next week, he'd leave. I helped him create a way to pitch his idea to Arthur."

"The ten-day experiment," Benji whispered.

"Scott said he'd do everything in his power to return in ten days. Arthur was devastated by the idea of losing a close friend, but ultimately, he knew the experiment would finally provide firm answers to anyone who questioned leaving. He believed Scott wouldn't survive the trip back. Everyone did, even Rebecca. She was an absolute wreck, a widow before his death."

"But you thought he'd make it, right?"

He chuckled lightly.

"*Right?*"

"Benji," Oliver said softly, "your dad never intended on coming back."

He covered his face with stiff hands. "Oh, god." His mind was racing a hundred miles an hour, and he couldn't keep up with them.

"The morning of the ten-day experiment, he stopped by the bank to deposit the same fifty-dollar bill." He shut his eyes. "That's when he said goodbye."

Benji's head was buzzing now. He tried to gather his thoughts into a sortable pile, but they slowly slipped into the abyss until his mind was blank. He could hardly focus as Oliver concluded the story.

"After ten days, the town was devastated. All of his friends needed someone to blame. Including your mom, Arthur, the Kois. The whole town, really. They needed a punching bag."

The room was cold.

"I don't know whether they had evidence I was involved or if they simply assumed I was. Either way, the fact was true. I helped Scott leave, and they found it fit that I stay far, far away. They wouldn't let me hurt anyone else. They wouldn't let me *kill* anyone else. So Arthur spoke to me on the thirteenth day. Said it'd be best if I moved into the abandoned house on Eudora. That I could quit my job. He would supply me with the money to live from, as long as I stayed out of everyone's way."

Benji shook his head.

"Listen to me," Oliver said. "This entire time I've lived here on this hill, I have never regretted my decision to help Scott leave. But I do regret that I didn't explain my actions better. Maybe if I did, I could have helped my friends deal with losing him. Maybe Arthur wouldn't hate me."

Benji gazed into his eyes, and although he tried, he couldn't look away. "I don't want you to go through the same thing. To have regrets."

"I'm fine with how things are." His answer required no thought. "I won't have any regrets."

"What about your friends? Your mother?"

Benji stared blankly.

Oliver dropped his chin. "I see."

"But really, thank you for telling me. It's nice to have answers for once." He gulped. "I'm sorry you had to go through that."

"I don't need any sympathy."

"Do you think you'll ever make up with them? Move back to town?"

"I don't know." He shrugged. "But that's enough about me. It's time you break out of this little rut you've hit."

"I think I already have." Benji stood, lifting a bucket in each hand. "I've got an idea."

A short boy stumbled through the square, swinging the buckets of paint in his hands to keep them from feeling too heavy. Townspeople stepped aside as he passed with a mischievous glare in his eyes.

Benji stopped at the front door of Ms. Camille's flower shop. A new window had been put in, and familiar flowers peeked through it, welcoming him. With a quick breath, he set the buckets on the walkway and stepped into the store.

Ms. Camille sat behind her counter, knitting. Her needles froze as the door shut behind him, and she raised her chin with a smile. Thankfully, there was no lipstick on her teeth this time. "Need some flowers for a girl?"

"Actually," Benji said, "I was wondering if you like green."

After some negotiation, he got started. Ms. Camille brought him a ladder from the back closet, and he popped open the paint cans to reveal a striking green.

When the brush first hit the bricks, Benji's hand shook. The obnoxious neon color left him laughing on the ladder. As silly as this idea seemed in his head, he was glad he went through with it. With every stroke of the brush over the gloomy building, he painted away his stress. He forgot about death. About time. All he thought about was green.

Ignoring the crowd of adults that had formed around his ladder, Benji pictured one of his old drawings, a silhouette of a town at night. At first he chose to leave it in shades of gray, but he eventually took the risk and attacked the page with bright watercolors. He decided he'd made a mistake, that he should have shaded it and left it at that. But the painting grew on him, and now it was one of his favorites.

Watching the building fade green in front of him, he imagined his dark gray sketch morphing into a bright image. Once you paint bricks, you can never go back. They can be painted over again, sure. But they can never revert to their natural brick color. It was the same as his drawing. He couldn't change his mind. He had to live with it.

All of Wishville would have to live with his choice today. Whether or not coloring the tiny building in the center of a blank canvas was a mistake, they had no say in the matter. This was a permanent change, and although small, it made Benji powerful.

He wasn't sure how long the painting took. By the time he finished, the crowd observing him had vanished, and the sun lie on the horizon. All Benji remembered while he worked was Ms. Camille emerging from inside the shop once in a while, biting her fingernails and facing the wet paint with raised brows. But once he had finished, stepped off the ladder, and observed his work, Ms. Camille handed him a cup of coffee from Seaside Cafe.

"You know, I have to admit that it's growing on me." She set her hands on her hips, gazing at the neon building of hers. "In fact, it might even help me with business."

Benji took a sip of coffee. It was bitter, not a drop of sugar inside, and he did his best not to pucker his lips. He forgot that Ms. Camille was a black coffee fan. "Thanks."

"I should be the one to thank you." She eyed his clothes. There were splatters of green all over his black sweatshirt, and his jeans had a few drips on them. "Look at you. You're a mess."

"I'm a mess in a lot of ways." Benji pulled at his sweatshirt, measuring the damage. "I think I kinda like it, though. Has an artsy feel."

Ms. Camille laughed with him. It was the first time he had a real conversation with the woman. Most of their interactions took place when Rebecca stopped by and he happened to be with her, or a quick *hello* on his way to Seaside Cafe on the rare occasion Ms. Camille stood outside. But today was different, and it was pleasant.

"Please, come in."

Benji shut the door behind them.

"You know, for a teenager you're not too bad." Ms.

Camille rushed around the room, searching for a worthy flower. She finally settled on a pot with a mustard yellow orchid and handed it to him. "Deliver this to Rebecca for me, will you?"

He grinned. "Of course."

"And if I may ask, where'd this idea come from?"

"Thought it'd be fun to spice up the square a bit."

"You're not doing this because you feel guilty for breaking my window, are you?"

Benji shook his head. "I swear—that was all Jett!"

"Oh, I'm just messing with you. Those Griffins are always causing problems. But you're quite the creative kid." She scooped her keys from the counter, preparing to lock the shop. "A lot like your father. We should both head home. It's getting late."

Before leaving the square, Benji stood by the fountain in the courtyard, observing his work.

"Interesting."

Mayor Perkins emerged next to him. He had a hand on his chin as he studied the neon building. "I heard you're responsible for this. Is that true?"

Benji didn't look at him. "I had permission from Ms. Camille. You can ask if you want. I wouldn't just paint it without—"

"I'm not accusing you of a crime." The mayor laughed. "I found it odd, that's all."

"Yeah it's a weird color."

"Have you and Sam made up lately?"

Benji tightened his grip on the pot.

"I hope you can forgive her for what she told us. Really, she did the right thing." Benji flinched as Mayor Perkins wrapped a hot arm around him. "Leaving town is dangerous. She only told us because she wants to keep you safe."

Benji stepped away as casually as possible, nearly running into the fountain. "I know."

"We forgive you for what you tried to do, and we know it won't happen again. But I still can't help but be concerned." He paused, and his carefree voice deepened. "Look, if something is going on with you, I want you to talk to me. The last thing I want is Sam or the others getting pulled into some kind of danger."

Benji forced himself to loosen his grip on the pot, worried about breaking it. "Danger?"

A gust of wind rushed past them, and the sky darkened a shade. They shivered in unison.

"You can't walk home in this weather." Mayor Perkins zipped his jacket. "Come on, I'll drive you."

Rebecca stood in the dining room when Benji arrived, arms crossed. He had already been expecting a lecture for coming home late, but when he shut the front door behind him, her face softened. "Your clothes." She eyed the paint splatters and smudges on his arms. "What happened to you?"

"I painted Ms. Camille's shop."

She uncrossed her arms, her stance loosening. "You painted what?"

"I painted the flower shop."

Rebecca backed away from him, collapsing into a chair. "Painted the shop."

"Are you mad?'

"No, of course not." She leaned over in her seat and rested her face in her hands. "But why?"

Something about Rebecca's reaction made Benji sick. He wanted her to lash out—to order him to his room and leave him in peace. But instead, she tried to understand him. And that was perhaps the scariest part

"Don't worry." Benji sat in the seat next to her. "I got permission first."

"That's not the point. I want you to tell me what's going on with you. You've been acting so strange lately."

He froze. "What do you mean?"

"I don't know. You seem . . . distant."

Benji wanted to tell her. He wanted to stand from his seat and scream that he wasn't okay. That in four days, he'd be dead. That in four days, this would all be over. He wanted to tell her that he couldn't accept the thought of dying. That he'd been trying to enjoy his last moments, but the pain of leaving the world behind kept him from sleeping. That he'd lost his appetite since he opened the envelope. That he didn't feel like himself anymore.

But instead, he leaned over to retie his shoelace. "That's weird."

Rebecca dropped her hands from her face. "I had this same feeling before your dad left."

He bit his cheek.

Your new friends are a lie.

Your paint is a lie

Your new colors are a lie.

Benji bit his cheek harder, trying to force the thoughts from running through his head. The thoughts he'd been suppressing for the last few days. The thoughts that haunted him as he lay restless in his bed at night. But no matter how much blood dripped inside his mouth, he couldn't keep the thoughts from flowing.

"Mom." Benji relaxed his jaw and pulled a smile, but his eyes were on the back wall. "Don't worry. I'm not going anywhere."

She shook her head. "You never told me you wanted to cut your hair."

"I didn't know I should have."

Your hair is a lie.

"And what was with that nightmare you had last night?"

Your dream is a lie.

"It was just a normal nightma—"

"You haven't had a nightmare like that since you were seven!"

Your life is a lie.

He folded his hands on his lap, crushing his fingers together until they were sore. "Relax, I'm fine." He wasn't sure who he was speaking to anymore—Rebecca, or himself.

She stared at him for a while, right into his untruthful eyes. Although his will ordered him to look away, he stared back. They held still, each waiting for the other to give in.

"Okay." There were bumps in Rebecca's voice. "Sorry. I don't know what I was thinking."

As Benji watched her feel the fabric of her sleeve, he couldn't keep his eyes from watering. He'd be leaving her soon. He'd have to say goodbye to the one person in town whose trust he valued most. Even if she didn't believe his story—even if she never understood him—the thought of leaving her frightened him. It hurt because she was trying. She was doing her best. But her best wasn't enough to keep him in Wishville.

Benji stood with another painful grin. "I better clean myself up." As much as he tried to feel guilty for his lies, he couldn't. The pride was overwhelming. Before this week, he had never been such a successful liar.

She pulled a loose thread from her sleeve.

"Goodnight, Mom." He could still taste the blood from his cheek. "I love you."

CHAPTER 20

liar

"Does Rebecca know you're here?"

"Told her not to bother me while I studied." Benji grinned. "She was overjoyed to give me some hours of peace."

"You tricky fool." Oliver shook his head with a stern look, but it dissipated with a dose of humor. He took a step back, holding the door open for Benji. "What are you standing for? Come inside."

Benji stood at the entrance of Oliver's home, trying to gather the right words. The man dropped his hand from the door handle and leaned against the wall inside. He was always great at giving Benji space.

Finally, the boy spoke. "Could we, maybe, stay out here today?" He turned around and took a seat on the highest step of the porch. The wooden boards crackled below him as Oliver shut the door and lowered his stiff body onto the wooden step.

Benji didn't look at him. He watched the waves twirl in the distance through the heaps of redwood trees ahead of them. The vague echo of a song filled the back of his head, a song the ocean danced to. A song he was soon to meet.

"What's on your mind?"

"Oh, I don't know." Benji peeled his focus from the tantalizing waves and instead observed how the long wisps of grass in the clearing shivered in the wind. "I guess I realized the world will go on without me."

"There's no fault in the fact."

"No, I guess not." Benji took a deep breath, finally gathering the courage to say what he had come here to say. "Oliver." He shifted himself in the man's direction with a weak grin. "I came here to say goodbye."

"Benji, you—"

"Really, I have to." His voice trembled, so he turned back to the evergreen trees. It hurt less that way. "Through all of this, you've been the only one to understand me. So, thank you. For everything."

Benji thought about how many needles each tree branch had, how many branches in a tree, and how many trees stood surrounding them. Then he shut his eyes, imagining how many grains of sand rested at the shore, how many droplets of rain filled the sea, how many insects were burying themselves into the dirt at that very moment.

"To think of how much there might be." Oliver gave him a telepathic stare, and the two simultaneously burst into laughter. It was Oliver who helped him understand himself. It was Oliver who helped him understand the world. And it was Oliver whom he would remember as his most faithful friend.

Once their humor died, he set a firm hand on Benji's shoulder. "Everything going according to plan?"

"Perfectly. Doesn't seem like anyone suspects anything." He fidgeted with his fingers. "I'll be leaving tomorrow."

Oliver smiled. "Good."

It was meant to be a peaceful silence, but it burned more than it soothed. Benji held back tears. There was no point in crying. One more day, and his life in Wishville would be dead and gone. All of this, everything that stood in front of him, it wouldn't matter anymore. Those tree needles, grains of sand by the shore, and burrowing insects would be as insignificant as his old life here in this tired town.

"I think I'm ready."

"You *think?*"

"I mean, I know." Benji nodded his head. "I *know* I'm ready."

"That's more like it."

They sat for a while longer on the porch steps. Two misunderstood men on top of an untouched hill. Two outcasts. Two crazies. They understood each other more than anyone else could. In a span of only a few minutes in the soft, salty wind, it was as though they had been speaking for hours. Enough had been said. This was the end.

This was goodbye.

Benji stood and offered Oliver his hand. He took it, using Benji's support to get back on his feet. Their eyes caught for only a fraction of a second before Benji witnessed him disappear. One blink ago he had stared at his back, and the next he was faced with nothing but a wooden door.

After waving softly at the old house, Benji stuck his

frost hands into the pocket of his sweatshirt and vanished in the trees of Eudora.

~

Benji believed this to be his last trip down Eudora Hill.

It was oddly eerie today. Twigs crunched beneath him
like bones in a cave. The sky was darker, and although
the moment with Oliver had been peaceful, he felt his
heart pounding. He went from walking to running, the
twigs crunching faster, wind smacking his face harder,
his legs reaching—

"Benji."

The voice had slipped into the air. Only a soft mum-
ble. He couldn't tell where it came from.

Benji froze, skidding across the dirt from his hasty
deceleration. Someone was here, on Eudora? That didn't
make sense. Curiosity burned him from the inside, but
fear overpowered him for once. After a deep breath, he
calmed his nerves and continued walking. *I'm imagining things.*

"Benji Marino?"

He curled his fingers into fists, but when he turned
around, his tense body relaxed. "What are you doing
here?"

"I could ask you the same." Chloe ran her hand
along the trunk of tree, feeling its bark. "Except I know
the answer."

"Answer?" Benji chuckled and shook his head. "I
felt like taking a hike, that's all."

"I knew it!" She ripped a piece of bark from the tree, still yet to look at him. "You can lie now."

Benji tucked his hands into his sweatshirt. It was getting colder. "Look, I really have to get home—"

"Before your mom realizes you snuck out the window?"

Benji glued his feet to the hill.

"I saw you come down from Eudora yesterday. With those buckets of paint. I know this isn't the first time you've *hiked* up this hill." She tossed the piece of bark in the air, and it fluttered down to Benji's feet. "You've been visiting Stricket."

Benji sighed. "I can explain."

"There's nothing to explain. You're letting him get into your head. I know he's the reason why you've been acting so weird lately. The reason you cut your hair. The reason you haven't been spending time with us. Don't you see what happened to you? You've gone crazy, just like Stricket."

"He goes by Oliver!" He loosened his jaw, realizing he had been clenching it. "We should both get home."

"You can't expect me not to tell anyone about this. At this rate, you're gonna get yourself killed." She tied her hair into a low ponytail. "Of all people, you should be the most afraid of him. He's the reason your father's dead."

"You don't know the full story."

Chloe scoffed. "I know enough." She broke into a jog down the hill, her boot heels amplifying the crunch of twigs.

This was the end. Benji could picture it already. He could see his mom standing over him with a broken face. He'd be stuck here forever. Stuck here *for his own good*. And for his own good, he would die here, right where he was born. The image was unbearable. No, he couldn't let this be the end.

He ran after her as fast as his legs would allow. "Wait!"

Their footsteps formed a steady beat. *Crunch. Clack. Crunch.*

"Please! I thought you could trust me."

She stopped, and Benji nearly fell trying to avoid running into her. He regained his balance, standing with heavy breaths.

"All I want is for the four of us to be together again." She faced him with red cheeks.

"Do you trust me?" Benji asked.

She kicked at a tree root.

"Chloe?"

"Yeah." She nodded. "Yeah, I trust you."

"Then please, don't tell anyone about this." He rubbed his arms, the cold reaching him again. "I'll stop talking to Oliver, okay? In a few days everything will go back to normal. I promise."

"Alright, deal." There was something foreign within her hazel eyes. A certain flair he couldn't understand. "But eventually, I'll be expecting an explanation from you."

"Thanks." The relief flooded him, but he didn't let it show. He walked down the hill, and after a few steps, glanced over his shoulder. "Oh, and Chloe?"

Her eyes caught his with a jolt, as if he had interrupted a lengthy trail of thought. "Yeah?"

"Goodbye."

CHAPTER 21

violin

Sam struck the bow against her violin with intense focus, but the notes she played were tangled and twisted beyond saving. She was playing underwater, playing while drowning, trying to keep herself afloat, trying to breathe, but failing. The notes were muted by the current. It was cold. Suffocating. Yet she kept playing.

Her neck tensed from the immense pressure on her chin rest. Her fingers were sore, burning. Flames among the waves. The more she played, the more the world disappeared. She no longer noticed the notes on the page or the scratching screams as the violin fought to articulate them. She fell deeper into the ocean, no longer flailing, but sinking. Lost beyond help.

She closed her eyes, and shadows engulfed her. Everything was gone now. Her worries, her anger, her confusion. It dissociated from her, sinking deeper than she floated in explosive mists. She could hear a distant squealing, but forced herself to tune it out. Instead, she focused on the darkness. It was comforting. Beautiful.

I wish I could stay here.

The door slammed open. Sam rose to the water's surface against control. The squealing of the violin intensified until she emerged, her eyes snapping open, and
the pain thundering back into her neck and fingers. She
could hear the violin again. It was screaming.

"Can you keep it down in here?"

Sam released her grip on the bow, and it tumbled
to the floor with a plop. Her fingers loosened on the
fretboard, stiff from the constant pressure, and the only
note that filled the room was that of deathly silence.
The image returned to her in a wave. Benji and James,
walking further away, fading into the distance. Chloe,
circling them frantically, looking for a missing solution.

Tobias stood in the doorway. He had a math book
opened in his hands, having run out of his bedroom
once the noise grew unbearable. But when Sam faced
him, he shut the book and pressed it gently against his
chest.

"Samantha!" Mayor Perkins emerged from behind
Tobias' shoulder. "What's going on with you?"

Sam set her violin on her bed and leaned over to
retrieve the fallen bow.

"There's no reason you should be playing that—"

"I think she needs some time to herself." Tobias
hugged his math book tighter.

"And you think you know what she needs more than
I do?"

"I think that—"

"You think you should get back to studying?" Mayor
Perkins nodded. "Yeah, that would probably be best."

Sam wished for Tobias' attention, but he was quick
to head back to his room. "Sorry," he said, and although

Sam was positive Tobias was speaking to Mayor Perkins, she liked to believe he said it for her.

She turned from the door, packing her violin back into its case. She hoped her dad would be gone by the time she finished, but when she lifted the case and set it on her desk, he was still standing in the doorway.

"Is this about Benji?"

"I don't wanna talk about it."

"Samantha," he said, "I don't think he's mad at you. And even if he is, I'm sure he knows you did the right thing."

She folded the music stand at the joints in an effort to be half-present. No, he had it wrong. It didn't matter if Benji was mad at her or not. She shouldn't have said anything. It was her fault that James didn't have his best friend to lean on. That Chloe lost someone who meant the world to her. And Sam had to watch this misery unravel, pretending she had nothing to do with it.

"You should be trying to communicate with him instead of taking your anger out on your family."

"I'm not!" Sam folded the music stand's legs against the main rod in a nasty slap.

"You better watch your—"

"Can't you leave me alone for once?" Sam chucked the folded stand onto the floor and turned away from him. She bit her lip to keep the tears from forming.

"Fine." He set his hand on the doorknob. "If that's what you want."

CHAPTER 22

message

Benji rubbed his eyes in the dining room, forcing alertness as best he could. He had trouble sleeping ever since he opened the envelope, and although it hadn't bothered him during school, it struck him the most during the weekend. He wasn't particularly sleepy, but the exhaustion was there. His legs were sore from soccer, and each step tortured his bruised feet. His eyes burned when he opened them in the mornings after a restless sleep. The days exhausted him. He found himself oddly irritable, clenching his fists whenever an old memory filled his mind.

Rebecca placed a palm over Benji's forehead, and he jerked himself away. She stepped away, waiting for him to speak for himself. When he didn't, she tossed in a clue. "Mr. Trenton phoned me this morning. Told me you left school early on Friday to call me."

Benji tried to panic, but no matter how hard he tried to tense his arms, they dangled like the limbs of a doll.

"But that's not the part that confuses me the most." Rebecca searched for his eyes. He avoided her. "He said you haven't been keeping up with your work."

"That's true," Benji said.

"Did something happen? Is this about how you tried to leave?" She pursed her lips and shook her head. "Why haven't you talked to me?"

"You never asked about it, so—"

"I love what you've been doing, Benji. I really do." There was a bumpiness to her voice. "But I can't help but feel concerned. Either you tell me what's going on now, or I might—I don't know if I'll be able to trust you anymore. You have to see where I'm coming from."

He wanted to shout that she'd never understand. That no matter how many stories he invented, she'd only believe the one she wanted to believe. But he knew that arguing with her would soil his plans. Today would be his last in Wishville, and it'd be best not to draw suspicion.

"I get why you're worried, but I'm not hiding anything." His feet ached from standing. "I've been bored with school, that's all."

"I booked you a meeting with a psychologist." The dullness in her eyes vanished, replaced with sharp, colorless blades. "Get ready. We're leaving in thirty minutes."

"Why?"

"I just—well—I know what's best for you." She blinked three times, restraining the knives of her eyes from reaching out to slash him. "Don't take it in a bad way. You deserve a chance to really talk with someone, you know? And if that person isn't meant to be me, then maybe I can accept that."

There was no rapid beating of his heart. No stiff

arms. No sweaty forehead. He was calm, and the lies slid off his tongue. Effortless. "Okay. I don't mind."

"What?"

"That's fine with me." He forced a smile. "It might help me."

She disarmed her eyes, and her forehead filled with creases. "I see. Well, I'm glad you're open-minded." She held her breath as she walked through the hall.

I got this. Benji nodded. *After I handle the meeting, I'll pack my things.*

His last morning in Wishville was spent in a shiny room at the end of Main Street. Benji had always pictured the building as a dreary place, but colorful rays of golden sun bloomed from the window. He was frustratingly comfortable, and he had to pinch his arm to keep his alertness from napping.

Dr. Atkins flipped through the paperwork Rebecca had filled for her. She skimmed the pages, placed it on the coffee table between their two seats, and adjusted her the white-framed glasses that made her hickory eyes glow. "Before we begin, I want you to understand that everything you say in this room is confidential." Dr. Atkins gestured to the clean space. "Nothing you say in this room will leave this room unless you share it yourself."

Benji wanted to smile. He wanted to curve his mouth and fool his way to the end, but he couldn't resolve the sense of failure that burdened him. He was in front of

Dr. Atkins, of all people! He never would've imagined himself in front of a psychologist. The last few days he'd been normal, concealing his dread of death with a charming grin and soft arms, but somewhere in his plan, he'd messed up.

It's okay. It's not over. Benji folded his fingers in his lap. *After I get through this meeting, I'll pack my things.*

"You're almost a high schooler." Dr. Atkins refolded the collar of her blazer. "How does that make you feel?"

She spoke with a voice of flowing cream. Benji considered the appeal. For the last few days, he'd been dying to talk to someone. He'd told Oliver everything, yet it wasn't enough to relieve himself. Multiple times he'd considered spouting the truth, but concealed it in fear that it'd ruin his plan to leave. But now Dr. Atkins sat in front of him, offering to listen and promising to keep a secret. The opportunity made him burst.

"I won't go to high school." His fingers tightened, and when he raised his head, colorful blotches on the hung canvases morphed into smothers of thick, black ink. The room grew hot. He felts wet forming under his sleeves. He had finally said it. The reality that he'd bottled inside him, he'd said it. He waited for the relief to crash into him, but instead, his body grew stiffer.

"Why don't we try something else?" Her tan skin and chestnut hair were the only colors that filled the room. The only things he could see. And Benji felt he could trust her.

Something about Dr. Atkins was familiar.

"You can ask me questions instead." Her eyes sparkled when they met with his, and he found himself smiling genuinely. "Does that sound better?"

His fingers loosened, and he adjusted his rotten posture. "Any kind of question?"

Dr. Atkins nodded. "Fire away."

Benji had never been skilled at solving puzzles. That was a task for James or Nina, but neither of them were with him at the moment, and he needed to solve this on his own.

"I heard she had a meeting with a child psychologist recently. The Kois were told she's been using her imagination as a coping method for her illness." Benji froze. That's what Rebecca had told him only a week before Nina died.

"Dr. Atkins," he said softly, "how many psychologists are there in Wishville?"

"Just me and Dr. Johnson, but he doesn't work with children."

"So you're the only child psychologist?"

"That's right."

His body clenched his jaw, warning him not to speak, but he ripped apart his teeth and let his voice slip out of his throat.

"Nina Koi was one of your patients," he said, "wasn't she?"

"I don't speak about my other clients." Dr. Atkins didn't flinch at the sight of his raging eyes. "Just how I'd never tell anyone what *you* tell me. So if there's something—"

"You need to understand. Nina's family is very close to mine." He stood. "I have to know if she told you anything. If you don't tell me, I won't be able to figure any of this out. I won't be able to know if—"

"If what she told you was true?"

The room paused.

Dr. Atkins' stiff persona dropped, and for a moment she was simply one of the few residents of Wishville. Her smile wavered, but she kept her gaze locked on him. "If you talk first, I might be able to help." She crossed her legs. "What exactly did Nina tell you?"

Benji sat. "She gave me an envelope with the date and time of my death."

"And you opened it."

"Yes." Benji gripped the fabric of his jeans. "Of course I opened it."

"I'll be right back." The room darkened as she passed the window, but the light returned as her feet left the rays illuminated on the carpet. She opened the bottom drawer of her desk. When Benji saw a glimpse of wadded papers and disorganized stationery, he almost laughed. Her calm, composed persona was all an act, not much different from Benji's.

Benji spotted a flash of red in her hand as she sat across from him. "Why don't we find out together?" She held an envelope in front of her, identical to the one Nina had given him. Benji froze.

"When Nina came in for the first time, she gave it to me. She said I'd know when to open it."

Benji pressed his back against the chair. The sweat on his palms were cold, and when he crossed his arms, a chill ran through his body.

"I'll open it first, okay?" Before Benji could say anything, her finger was stuck into the crease of the envelope. After a blink, it was open.

She peeked inside before offering the envelope to Benji.

Pure danger traced his fingertips for the second time. He hardly made contact with the envelope, holding it tenderly. Before committing, he glanced at Doctor Atkins. She nodded, and he reached inside. A paper slipped out in a hurry, escaping its prison. The job was almost halfway done. He was about to unfold it, but a stronger curiosity stopped him.

"Did she say anything before she gave it to you?" he asked.

Dr. Atkins smiled, although it wasn't a stable one. "She told me it would help a friend understand." She nodded her head, encouraging Benji to proceed.

He unfolded the paper and leaned forward, reading Nina's message.

"But I *don't* understand." Benji squinted at the page. Two words. They didn't change.

Not today.

"Does it mean anything to you?"

"No." Benji tossed the page onto the coffee table and sighed. "It means nothing."

The ticking of the wall clock filled the room.

Benji ran his hands through his hair. "What am I supposed to understand?" With each tick of the clock, the pain in his head grew thicker.

Dr. Atkins cleared her throat. "Benji, this is only an idea, but have you ever considered the possibility that," she paused, "maybe Nina couldn't really tell the future?"

Benji peeled his hands from his head.

"I can't share information about my other patients, but I *can* tell you that supernatural powers don't exist. Sometimes kids play pretend."

"But there were so many signs that—"

"You can collect evidence to support any claim, no matter how ridiculous it is. It doesn't mean you're unintelligent. Even geniuses can be fooled into believing ridiculous notions. Luckily, Wishville's strong. We spread the truth, so everyone can stay on the same page. But what happens when someone sides with a different view?"

Benji didn't respond, so she answered for herself. "It's frightening, Benji. It's frightening when people are too curious. When they talk about things that aren't really talked about." She leaned forward slightly, smiling broadly. "It's perfectly natural to be curious. It's what leads you to facts. But sometimes those facts aren't true. You've got to understand that."

Every time she paused to breathe, the ticking of time haunted Benji again.

"I have evidence." He spoke so fast that his words jumbled together like tangled yarn. "She told me when she'd die, and she was right."

"When did she predict it?"

"The day before."

"There's many cases of people who predicted when they'd die. Sometimes people can sense when they're reaching the end. It's instinctive."

"What if she didn't have that *feeling*? What if she actually knew?"

"Have you considered something called a coincidence?"

"I swear, she could tell the future!"

Dr. Atkins nodded. "Okay." More nodding. "I see what you mean. Yes. And from talking with you today

I have a feeling I know what's going on." She paused, waiting for Benji to look at her. "Sometimes your brain changes what you remember in order to support what you want to believe. Be honest with yourself. Do you *want* to believe Nina could tell the future?"

Benji thought on that for a little. For some time. A long time. He closed his eyes. Messed with his fingers. Bit his tongue. In the end, he found himself nodding. *I don't want to believe Nina had something wrong with her.*

"Do you think that might be the reason why you allow yourself to be so easily convinced of something that goes against science?" She pointed to the envelope. "If after reading the message we opened today, you still don't understand, I don't see why you would think there *is* something to understand. Do you think these beliefs you have are healthy?"

His sore muscles grew so tense they went numb. He observed the room, remembering where he was. The thoughts rushed back to him. *I'm at a psychologist's office. My mom sent me here. She thinks I'm crazy.* His face boiled. He wasn't sure where the anger came from, but it did, and he wished to scream.

Am I going crazy like Nina? He grabbed his head in different places, hoping he could reach a conclusion. *Or am I the only person in this town who's actually sane?*

CHAPTER 23

pitch

Every other Sunday night, Stricket would drive to the convenience store in the square for his staple groceries. Today was Chloe's chance to take action. Perhaps the *only* chance where she'd have enough willpower to pull through with it.

With a bag from the supply closet hauled over her shoulder, Chloe hiked up Eudora Hill for the second time in her life. Although her calves burned and her neck ached from the pressure of the bag, it was another pain that encouraged made her stop. "I'm doing this for Benji." The bag slipped as her fingers loosened, but she tightened them and continued walking. "I can fix this."

Yesterday, Benji had verified the connection between him and Stricket. Chloe had heard the stories before. Stricket was crazy. He infected Benji's mind with his cold lies. It must have been *him* who was responsible for Benji planning to leave earlier this month. It would explain all of it. Benji's peak of curiosity. His odd questions. Why he cut his hair, made new friends, and sat motionless in class. Stricket was the puppet-master behind it all, and Chloe was here to cut the strings.

Chloe watched her boots as she walked, avoiding any rocks or twigs that might cause her to slip. When a vibrant green replaced the dull dirt below her, she paused and raised her chin to face a house standing boldly on the hill. A darkness filled the windows. The lights were off.

She stepped back, removing her foot from the grass clearing. The moonlight shimmered down like a spotlight, and she'd rather stay in the shadows of trees. With a fluid motion, she threw the equipment bag off her shoulder. Out rolled twenty-three baseballs. They spread around her feet, prevented from rolling by strange dips in the dirt.

Chloe leaned over and delicately lifted one of them. She adjusted her form, ready to throw. She yearned for for someone to snatch her hand and tell her not to do it. She yearned to scoop the baseballs back into the bag and return them to their rightful home in the equipment closet. For Stricket to come home from shopping before she could take action.

But there was nothing to stop her.

It was not a surge of inspiration that made her throw. Not a brilliant decision crafted in her mind. What made her throw weren't her thoughts, but her lack of them. Her mind empty, all that filled her was a raging emptiness that filled her muscles. The baseball whirled through the inky air, crashing through a window by the door.

As the glass shattered, Chloe grabbed another baseball. She gave it a quick bounce in her hand before sending it flying through a different window. It rung as it hit something inside. Double points.

"I'm doing this for Benji," Chloe reminded herself. Her eyes watered, but her head was too warm for tears.

She wasn't tracking how many she'd thrown, but eventually, she ran fingers along the dirt and found nothing but an empty bag. Her fury settles, and as she saw the broken house, she bit her lip and turned away. She was afraid of the damage. Afraid of what she'd done.

She kicked a tree, and her toes throbbed from the impact.

It was at the same time Chloe had climbed back through her bedroom window when Benji slipped out of his. His backpack was filled with a few more items than his last attempt. One to-go bowl from Chowdies, two crinkled bills, and a change of clothes. He trekked through the outskirts of town, making sure no one could spot him.

Yet even if an old friend were to see him, what would be the harm? They were no longer in his way. Benji knew that this time, there would be no one to stop him. No Chloe to chase him. No Sam to laugh in his face. No James to block his path. It would only be him, alone at the edge of Wishville.

Nearly two days until the 23rd. Two days to live outside of town. To Benji, that was enough.

He reached Candy Road faster than he thought he would. Everything moved rapidly, and before he could bat an eye, he stood facing the *LEAVING WISHVILLE* sign for the second time this month.

There was no staring at the lights of town and waving

goodbye. No watching of the seagulls and listening to the waves for the last time. Instead, he powered toward the exit. He was ready to leave everything behind. School, his mom, all of his old friends, classmates, Oliver. He was ready to let go of it all, and spend his last two days discovering the one mystery he had left.

He brought his foot forward to step off the bridge, but it came plummeting back. *Don't do it.* His mind spoke to him with a voice louder than his urge to leave.

"I'm getting out of here." Benji tried to move, but his feet remained bolted to the ground. He relaxed his arms, restraining himself from battling the energy that kept him still. The end was so close, yet miles away.

"Why?" Benji stepped further from the border, retreating from the bridge. "Why can't I leave?"

The sign didn't answer him, so he searched his brain for a reason. A single message wiggled its way from his mind to his lips, sliding off his tongue.

"Not today."

His eyes widened, to two moons resting on his nose.

It was a warning. Nina had told him not to leave town. His own conscience stopped him from taking the last steps away from everything he knew. Benji understood that tonight wasn't the right time to leave, even with only two days left on the clock. The only question was *why?* He had done everything he needed to, hadn't he?

Part III

home

CHAPTER 24

jett

It was Monday, May 22nd, and Benji stood in the hall of Wishville Junior High. As kids gave him high-fives or stared from a distance with narrowed eyes, he couldn't help but wonder why he was still here. Tomorrow was his death day. He should have been miles from Wishville by now, but here he was, living this new life he created as if he planned to stick with it from the beginning.

"What's up, Benji?" Ray bumped into his arm and walked next to him. "Why weren't you here this morning?"

Benji hadn't bothered showing up early. Soccer was the last thing on his mind, and even school wasn't one of his highest priorities. If Rebecca hadn't knocked on his door this morning, he probably could have slept through the entire day.

"You doing okay?"

Benji ignored him. The school was gray.

He left Ray behind him in the hall, entered Mr. Trenton's class, and dumped himself into his familiar seat. Although Benji radiated a fresh dullness, the students were too stuck in their own world to notice. James rolled his pencil across his desk, a sign of boredom, but he refused to read for stimulation. He willed himself to stay present, to make sitting in Mr. Trenton's class and being in Mr. Trenton's class the same activity. Sam, on the other hand, did everything in her power to mentally escape. She hummed, pinching her arm whenever she found herself listening to the room's ambiance. She forced a song out of her, a song she wished to live in.

"Are you okay?"

Benji jumped at Mr. Trenton's voice, raising his chin to the board. However, his teacher's focus was not on him, but Chloe.

"Sorry." She crossed her arms, pressing them against her stomach. "I'm not feeling well."

"Something must be going around." His eyes trailed over Benji as he pointed to the door. "Why don't you see the nurse?"

"I'm fine." Chloe unraveled her arms, opened her binder, and lifted a pen.

The class erupted with whispers. As Mr. Trenton scribbled notes on the blackboard for them to copy down, Peyton sat sideways in her chair, facing Noah. "Think she feels bad for him?" She held her palm against her cheek in attempt to shield her voice from the rest of the room.

Noah laughed through his nose with unsteady breaths, keeping himself quiet. "Baseball or not, he's a jerk."

Their efforts to remain quiet failed. "You don't have to be mean about it." Audrey peeked at the board, ensuring Mr. Trenton had his back to her before turning her head in their direction. "But I agree it wasn't right."

The chattering of classmates filled Benji's mind until he couldn't decipher words from each other. It mushed together, like listening to a poem from underwater. His neck jolted in crazy directions, but it was pointless. Even Jett couldn't handle it. He held his hands over his ears until he burst, spinning around to face Sam's desk.

"You hearing this, Perkins?"

The chattering stopped. Everyone faced Jett, waiting. For the first time in six days, Benji was too confused to care about leaving town.

Sam frowned, her humming interrupted. "That wasn't cool of you."

"Me? It could've easily been Noah, and no one would've suspected it." Jett didn't bother lowering his voice anymore, and apparently, neither did Noah.

"You think I'd do something like that?" Noah's eyes simmer behind smoking glasses. "It doesn't even have to be someone on the baseball team. It could be—"

"Who else would know how to access the supply closet?"

"Obvious you know." Noah scoffed. "Asking that question is the same as accusing yourself."

"Not more than it's accusing you."

Mr. Trenton slammed a piece of chalk onto his desk. "I know you're upset about the incident, but there's no proof any of you did it. If you have any *real* evidence on who it could've been, I suggest you let me know *in private*." He grabbed his chalk, adding onto the growing list of notes. "Whoever it was, they had no right vandalizing Oliver's property, no matter what rumors might be spreading through town."

Benji stood. "Oliver?"

Mr. Trenton's hand paused over the blackboard.

Benji abandoned his things, racing for the door.

"Benji, don't—"

He burst into the hall and ran to the front door. With all the strength left in his body, he ran to Eudora Hill. He had visited Oliver so many times now that the journey was innate to him, and in what felt like seconds, he approached the clearing.

A clicking filled the air, mesmerizing the trees of Eudora into a dreary sleep. Each step made Benji shiver, as though walking through the path of a ghost. The higher he traveled, the more prominent the clicking noise attacked him. He reached the clearing. He could see the noise now. Hammering.

As he dragged himself across the clearing, he watched Oliver pound rusty nails into the wood of his home. He stood on a stool, a hammer in one hand, pressing a piece of wood with the other. Benji almost couldn't recognize the place. The shattered windows and splintery boards intruded the magic of the hill. The grass beneath him turned brown, the trees a dark gray, and the sky a menacing white—bright enough to blind.

Benji waited for his hands to go stiff, but nothing came. A fear passed through him—a fear that for the rest of the day, nothing had the power to faze him.

He stepped closer. His head jotted left and right, unsure of which bruise to focus on. They were equally painful.

"Your windows," Benji said.

Oliver gave nothing more than a slight flinch at Benji's voice. He hammered at the wood louder than before, but this time, he missed every nail.

"Oliver?"

He pounded louder.

Benji's focus caught to the shimmering shards of glass on the dirt. Among them was the occasional baseball. He leaned over to grab one and tossed it into the air. The fabric was rough, nearly bursting at the seams. He caught the ball and rolled it between his fingers. Looking closely, he saw three words printed in green.

Wishville Junior High.

Benji walked along the deck, observing every ball he could find. Each one had the same writing. He tossed the ball to the ground in rage and turned the corner, approaching Oliver with a raspy voice. "Why would they do this?"

The man stopped pounding, but he froze fazing the wall of his house.

Oliver, I—"

"Why the hell are you here?"

Benji shook his head. "You know I—"

"Don't play dumb with me." He gave the wood one last knock before hopping off his stood and tossing his hammer onto the dirt. "You're all a bunch of filthy liars. All of you."

Oliver walked away, leaving his work unfinished. Benji tried chasing him, but Oliver cut him off with a rigid turn, towering over Benji from the highest step of his deck. "You were supposed to leave last night." His nose twitched. "I believed in you."

Benji gulped. "You know I'd never do this."

"I don't give one damn who did it!" He huffed. "I'm not mad about my windows, Benji."

As Benji watched Oliver enter his tattered home, a

twinge of hope leapt away from him. He jumped to grab it, clinging to it like he was mad. With a deep breath, he spoke to the man's back. "You still believe me, don't you?"

It couldn't be true. After all they'd been through? After how much they've shared?

The man stopped at the doorway, glancing at Benji through the corner of his eye. There was a spark between them, a familiar glow, but as Oliver set his hand on the knob, it faded.

Benji stood blankly at the base of Oliver's deck. His worry shifted into rage. Someone had come here to hurt Stricket, and in doing so, they took away the one person who understood him. The one person he could trust with anything. Who could possibly do this?

But when he remembered the scattered baseballs and broken glass, the culprit couldn't be more clear.

Chloe couldn't keep her foot from tapping. Benji ran out of class. He must have been angry. Infuriated. Although Mr. Trenton continued the lesson, his students couldn't forget about Benji's explosion. In less than a week, the average boy in class morphed into someone they admired, someone they were concerned for. Chloe caught Audrey peeking at the door, and Jett asked Mr. Trenton if he planned to alert the office. Everyone agreed it was wrong not to acknowledge that he left class, and probably school campus, but Mr. Trenton responded with a simple, "Let him be," and that was the end of it.

No matter how much Chloe tried to support her actions, she knew it wasn't right. The conspiracies rushing through class were enough to crush her soul. It was only a matter of time before they'd narrow the list of suspects to her. They would find out. They all would.

What do I do? Her foot tapped faster, and she bit her pencil eraser.

The bell rang for lunch. Jett and Noah argued on their way out, blaming each other for the incident. Audrey followed James, blabbering about her little sister's piano recital. Sam's hair fizzed in the air as she dashed from the room, her theory notebook tucked in an iron grip. And as Chloe watched her classmates walk away—the classmates she'd gone to school with for nearly nine years—she felt like she didn't know these people.

By the time she left class, a herd of students had gathered on the right side of the hall, opposite the cafeteria. Peyton rushed past her, slamming into her shoulder without an apology. The golden locks she called *natural* loosened as she ran. It was the first time Chloe had seen Peyton run outside of PE, so she followed after her, curious.

The herd formed a tornado of shouts and shoves. After fighting her way through the crowd a bit too forcefully, she emerged from the front in time to see Benji shove a fist into Jett's jaw.

Jett skimmed the locker doors before regaining his balance and locking his eyes on Benji. Standing in the spotlight of a growing crowd, a grin swept over his lips. He rubbed the side of his face as though he'd only been flicked.

Peyton's frown lifted with a dose of glowing

excitement. There hadn't been any school fights since Oliver was in high school, so the thrill of witnessing one overpowered concern of the consequences. A part of Chloe hated herself for wanting to see the fight. Jett stood nearly a foot taller than Benji and was blessed with a build that could easily crush him. The winner was obvious. Yet at the same time, Chloe clung to the doubt that maybe Benji was stronger than she thought.

But when Benji faced the crowd, Chloe stopped smiling. She backed away, stepping onto someone's foot. "Sorry!" He breathing sped, and her soul sunk in a punctured ship. Benji wasn't normal. He wasn't forcing a grin. From the look in his eyes, he wasn't thirsty for answers. It was the first time she had spotted him with nothing but pure rage between his gritted teeth.

Jett's hair shimmered in the hallway lights, flopping on his head as he leapt closer to Benji. "You wanna pick a fight with *me*?" He took his right arm and flung it behind his back. "If you want, I can even out the competition." From the looks of it, the opportunity of crushing Benji in battle was something he'd always longed for. The punch had hardly shaken him, and he saw the event as more of a sparring joke than a real fight.

Benji sent his arm flying from his side. Jett stepped away smoothly, and the short boy's fist slammed against the cold lockers. He pulled his throbbing hand away with a wince, glaring at Jett as he shook the numbness out of his fingers.

Jett looked down at Benji again, not in humor or anger, but in shock.

The room froze. Students finally understood that Benji wasn't bluffing. He wasn't playfully fooling around. This time, he had actually gone insane. The admiration the school had given him for all the change he'd created—it dissipated with a blink.

"Jeez, what the hell's your problem?" Jett held his hands in front of him. "I'm not trying to kill you. I mean, I definitely could. But I'm not trying to."

Benji narrowed his eyes and took a step forward. The crowd filled with murmurs, many considering to interfere, but none taking action. What was the correct way to act as spectator of a fight? They had never studied such a scenario before.

"You're insane!" Benji peeled back his arm once again, but when he reached out to punch, his back slammed into the lockers, and his arm flopped back to his side. Someone had given him a gentle shove from the side, but it was enough to throw his momentum off.

"Seriously?" Sam stood a few steps ahead of the crowd, her cheeks redder than her hair.

Benji forced himself away from the lockers, not bothering to look at her. The only person he could see in the room was Jett, who had now lowered both of his hands. His eyes glowed with a fiery mahogany hue. They were burning. "Never thought Marino had a violent side." His voice was deeper than Chloe remembered it being. Benji's aggression had transformed the careless jokester into a madman.

"Stop, both of you." Sam took a step between them. "This is stupid."

"Both of us?" Jett grabbed her by the shoulder and shoved her into the clump of students behind her. "It's your *boyfriend* here who started this."

Sam stumbled backwards, running into Noah, who

helped stop her from falling. She rubbed her sore arm, and Noah fixed his crooked glasses. As Benji and Jett shot after each other, students trickled between them, shouting and blocking their path. Chloe watched the chaos unfold from the edge of the hall, the last to remain where the crowd had once stood.

Jett struggled wiggling through the wall that had formed in front of him. "Let me through!" He clawed through the students, but each layer he penetrated reformed instantly.

Benji leaned forward, but was pulled back by strong arms. "Calm down!" Noah said.

"You took away the one person who believed in me!" Benji was screaming at Jett, but his voice was loud enough to be heard in all of Wishville.

Chloe held her breath as the realization struck her. The pieces came together in her mind, and she leaned over, a sickness punching her stomach.

"You know what?" Jett gave up on reaching Benji. He paused, staring over the blockade. "You're crazy, Marino."

"You don't know anything about me!" Benji's voice made Chloe's head spin. The same image circulated her mind until she nearly fell from dizziness. She saw herself with a baseball in hand, a sack over her shoulder. She heard the clashing of windows echo through her brain, encouraged by her seething rage. Her forehead ached. "I *do* know you," she whispered, but when the words spilled from her mouth, she was guilty for lying.

"*You don't know me.*" Benji's voice looped through Chloe's head. "*You don't know anything about me!*"

The shouts were directed at Jett, but they swung at a sharp angle to jab her.

Chloe backed toward the opposite end of the hall, disconnecting herself from the scene. She spun around, her silent footsteps vibrating through the floor, leaving the mess she'd created behind her. Trying to forget it.

"I guess maybe I don't."

CHAPTER 25

sugar

It must have been the first time in history where Jett was no longer the one to blame. He'd been sent to class with nothing but a lecture and a red slip for his parents, while Rebecca was phoned to retrieve Benji from the main office. As initiator of the fight, his suspension was to last three days, and upon return he'd be on strict watch by the teachers. Supposedly they also decided the time off would be a perfect chance for him to work on missing assignments, hence the giant stack of papers on his lap.

There was not one exchange of words in the car. Rebecca wasn't sure what to say or ask. She had been concerned for Benji the past two weeks, but when she looked at him now, she radiated with frustration. There had to be a reason for his odd behavior. The fact that he refused to tell her only caused her worry to grow. What kind of burden could he not share with his own mother?

That afternoon—the afternoon of May 22nd—Benji had tucked himself into his room, set on sleeping the rest of his life away.

Rebecca sat alone at the dining room table with a sore forehead and a glass of wine in hand.

A knock came from the door, but before she could stand, the visitor had already burst inside. Mayor Perkins shut the door behind him and crossed his arms. "I heard the news."

While she made evening coffee for them to binge on, he explored the living room. "I'm glad to see you're starting to embrace the sunshine." He admired the opened blinds and pulled-back curtains.

"You can go ahead and shut them if you want." Rebecca took two cups from the cupboard. "It'll be late soon."

"Then you should enjoy the sun while it's still out." He entered the dining room, satisfied. "Where's Benji?"

Rebecca filled their mugs with coffee. "His room. Asleep." She retrieved a jug of milk from the fridge and poured a generous blob into each cup. "Sorry, out of cream."

He shrugged. "It'll do."

They sat at the table, warm mugs in hand. "I understand your concern." Mayor Perkins took a sip and puckered his lips. "Scott was the same way. Before he left town for the ten-day experiment, he was acting the same as Benji. Perfectly normal—perhaps better than normal." He snuck to the sugar container by the fridge and helped himself to a few heaping tablespoons. "I'm worried he may end with a similar fate. Or worse."

"What do you mean, *worse*?"

The mayor closed the lid and spun around, leaning his weight on the edge of the countertop. "What I mean is that Benji needs to be on close watch." He sipped his modified coffee and grinned. "And I also recommend you book meetings with Dr. Atkins more frequently."

Rebecca watched the coffee swirl in her cup.

"Sam nearly screams when I mention his name. If none of the kids can tell us what's going on, we need to take action for the worst. Imagine if Benji were to be gone one day. They'd be crushed. *We'd* be crushed. Don't let him follow the same path as Scott."

Rebecca shook her head. He had a meeting with Dr. Atkins only two days ago, and following the event nothing had changed. If anything, he had grown worse. She couldn't possibly force him through that again.

"Do you want him to do something crazy? You better book—"

Rebecca slammed her mug on the table, her forehead filled with creases. "He's not your son, okay?"

The mayor waited a moment, but when he spoke again, his voice was as soft and charming as ever. "I know he's not my son." He propelled himself from the countertop and stood firm. "But I made a promise I'd keep everyone in town safe. That applies to Benji whether he's my son or not."

Rebecca loosened her grip on the mug. The creases in her forehead relaxed, her mind allowed to function again. "You're right. I'll do that." She set the cup down and scooped her purse from the seat of the chair next to her. "I suppose we should both head back to work?"

Mayor Perkins didn't stand. "You're gonna leave him here? Alone?"

Rebecca froze. He was right, but she couldn't afford to stay at home for the next two weeks. A face flashed in her mind, and she smiled. "I think I know who to call."

CHAPTER 26

babysitter

Benji woke to the sound of shuffling papers. Once the realization seeped in, he sprung from his bedsheets with eyes wider than the mood. Lauren stood by his open desk drawers, flipping through empty worksheets and failed quizzes. He was too confused to question her.

"Don't worry, I always slacked at the end of the year too." She tossed his assignments back into his dresser and grinned. "Guess who's your babysitter again?"

Benji froze as the wall clock told him it was nearly four. "What day is it?" He reached to pull at his hair, forgetting he had cut it too short to do so. "Lauren? The date?"

"It's still Monday." She leaned against the wall. "Rebecca wanted me to come watch you before going back to work."

His head flopped back onto the pillow in relief. "Why exactly are you here?"

"They think something strange is going on with you. In other words, they think you're crazy." Lauren swiped two pages from the top of his desk and held them in the air. One was the paper from Nina, and the other was a calendar with May 23rd circled in red. "What exactly is it you're planning?"

Benji closed her eyes, trying to block Lauren out, but she whacked him with a pillow to knock him back into Wishville. "Wake up!" She hit him again.

He stood and snatched the pillow from her before flinging it across the room. "Will you stop that?"

"Not until you explain yourself."

He groaned.

"Stop being lazy!" She tossed a second pillow into his arms and left the room, slamming the door behind her.

Benji tried to wrap his mind around the fact that tomorrow night, he'd be facing his death. It was already the twenty-second, and he hadn't left town yet. *Should I leave now?* After a moment of thought, he shook his head. There had to be a reason why Nina told him not to leave the other night. Why he couldn't cross the bridge. But besides Jett's ignorant move against Oliver, nothing significant had changed. Something was missing.

Benji eventually entered the dining room to find Lauren sighing at the refrigerator. "No cream?"

He shrugged. "Just use milk."

"What are you, a caveman?" She retrieved the carton with pursed lips.

Lauren brought Benji a cup of coffee and sat next to him at the dining room table. He had always been more comfortable with Lauren than other adults, who always sat across from him as if he had knives protruding from his sides. She was the big sister he never had, although he'd never dare tell her that. Sipping coffee with her at the table, it took all of his willpower to restrain himself from telling her. He could feel the words slipping his tongue, but when he opened his mouth, they retreated into the depths of his throat and locked themselves there.

Lauren didn't say a word. She stared at the wall silently, giving him space. He appreciated her silence. She didn't bombard him with a billion overwhelming questions.

The clock ticked.

"Would you believe me," he said, "if I told you I'm gonna die?" The guilt flooded him. *No*, he thought, *I can't tell her.* He wished to pop the words like bubbled in the air. If Oliver, the craziest man in town, no longer believed him, what chance did Lauren?

"Well, we're all gonna die." She stopped laughing when she caught his expression. "Does this have to do with the 23rd?"

"Huh?"

"You know, from those papers earlier."

"Oh uh—well—" Benji took a deep breath. "It's for a science test. Gotta write reminders or I'll forget all about it." It no longer burned to lie.

"So what do mean by dying?"

"Huh?" Benji shrugged off his grin. "Don't remember that."

"The adults—I think—well—I have a feeling they think you're gonna commit suicide. Or leave town or something. I don't know."

"What?"

"You've drawn too many suspicions." She sighed. "Look, you don't have to tell me anything, but I'm pretty sure I know what this is about. Rebecca told me you and James don't even talk anymore."

Benji stared at the table.

"It always sucks when friends fall apart." After a final sip, she set her mug on the table. "You don't have to pretend you're okay with it. No one should."

He remembered Oliver, picturing him staring through a broken window at the top of Eudora, watching everyone's lives run by as he sat frozen from afar. *"I don't want you to go through the same thing. To have regrets."*

"Actually, you're right." Benji paused. "Ever since Nina died we've been falling apart. And it's all because of me. I was too worried about my own problems to care." He told Lauren about his first escape plan. How Sam ratted him out about trying to leave. He was about to share why he jumped at Jett earlier today, but managed to stop himself in time. He wouldn't tell her anything related to Nina or Oliver. That information was too dangerous to mess with. But even with limited knowledge, perhaps she could help. "And what happened today . . . I don't know. I haven't been myself lately."

Lauren's face took a twisted form, and her neck went stiff. "It's always hard when a friend passes away." She forced a smile. "But that doesn't mean you can make up stories and get into fights. How's that gonna solve anything? You should try talking to them. Explaining yourself."

Benji pushed his coffee away from him, fully focusing on Lauren.

"Don't give up yet," she said. "You can fix this."

In that moment, the last piece to the puzzle came flying back at him. The reason why he hadn't been able to leave town had nothing to do with Nina *or* his death. He needed to fix the mess he created, first. Once he could bring everyone back together, he'd be ready. He could finally leave it all behind him.

"I'll help you out as long as you promise not to do anything *too* crazy."

"I won't." Benji smiled. "Promise."

"You should get changed into something nicer." She pointed to the hall. "Leave this little friendship quarrel to me."

After changing into fresh clothes, Benji realized how messy his room had become. Clothes layered the floor like moss, bed sheets melted off the mattress, and his new stack of assignments he'd been sent home with earlier today had been crammed under his desk, as if storing it near a working space made it less sinful. Although he didn't understand the reasoning with only one day left, he spent a portion of his meager time organizing. Put his clothes in the laundry. Made his bed. Stacked the school work he'd never do on the edge of his desk. When his room was back to its usual scale of messiness, he sat in his chair and analyzed the calendar page Lauren had pulled out earlier. It was crazy to think it was already the twenty-second. One more day and everything would be over. All of it. The idea didn't particularly scare him anymore. Instead, he laughed. He had been suspended for three days, but could only make two of them.

He double-checked the year on Nina's letter. Nope, he hadn't mistaken it. Tomorrow night, at exactly eleven-fifty-nine, he'd be dead.

A knock from the bedroom door interrupted his thoughts. In his earliest memories of Lauren, she had always been the type of burst into rooms without notice. He frowned at his desk. "Yeah?"

But when the door opened, it wasn't her.

Sam stared at the carpet as she stepped inside. "Lauren phoned me earlier. Said you needed to tell me something?" She raised her chin.

Benji sighed. *Lauren's crazy.*

"Benji?"

"Oh—uh—yeah." He stood. "That's true. You see, I think I'm ready to explain the truth. The right way, and all of it."

Sam leaned against the wall. "And how, exactly?"

"Let's meet at Blueberry one last time."

Sam crossed her arms. She wasn't convinced.

"You have to trust me." Benji peeled his eyes away, remembering how strange his behavior must have been lately. "Yeah, guess that's a lot to ask when I've been acting like a complete lunatic."

"A complete idiot."

"Yeah, a complete idiot." Benji hopped onto his bed, his feet dangling off the edge. "But trust me. I'll explain everything."

Sam tapped her feet, humming in thought. "Sure," she said. "Okay, let's meet at Blueberry. But this is the last time."

Benji smiled.

"After you come back to school, we'll talk to them about meeting up." Benji's smiled faded, and Sam frowned. "What?"

"Any chance it could be today?"

"Today?"

He nodded.

"That's impossible. Your mom won't even let you leave the house." Sam raised her voice. "You're fourteen, and Lauren is literally babysitting you again."

"You don't understand." He shook his head. "There's only two days left."

"Two days left for what? That's not enough time, and I'd have to figure out how to invite everyone, myself. Why does it need to be in two—" Her eyes locked to a calendar sitting on his desk, and Benji immediately stood in front of it. "Wait. Why is the twenty—"

"Sam, please." Benji stepped toward her. "I'll explain everything at Blueberry, but we need to meet soon."

She stared at him with vacant eyes, her soul trapped in the depths of her mind, sorting through her thoughts. When her presence returned, her eyes filled with a nostalgic glow. "Tomorrow at six-thirty. We can pick blueberries then." She spoke fast. Urgently.

"Six thirty?" Benji's arms went stiff. "Can you make it earlier?"

"Do you want my help or not?"

Benji relaxed his arms, exhaling through his mouth. "Okay." He knew he couldn't push it any further. "Six-thirty."

"Six-thirty," Sam echoed.

"And you think James will come?"

"Don't worry." She propelled herself off the wall with a smirk. "I'll make him."

A rush of heat filled his head, but it vanished with a cool breath. For a quick moment, Wishville stopped. The break from time was peaceful, and Benji wished it could last forever. But when Sam cleared her throat, the ticking continued. "I should go."

"Sam." Benji hopped off his bed, and she peeked over her shoulder. "Thanks for this."

"It's fine." Her shoulders tensed. "Let's just—I don't know—call it even."

Before Benji could ask what she meant, Sam was gone.

He smiled at the empty doorway before collapsing onto his freshly-made bed. The air was warm as he watched the ceiling, his thoughts running wild. He dreaded tomorrow, yet at the same time, he couldn't wait.

CHAPTER 27

invitation

I t was Tuesday, and Chloe decided to sit with Jett for lunch. She wasn't particularly sure why, since only yesterday he was in a fight with one of her closest friends. Perhaps she held no grudge against him because she knew he wasn't at fault.

"You've got some weird friends," Jett said. "Don't you, Mortimer?"

"Yeah, I had some weird friends." She poked at her sandwich. It was useless to try and fix their friendship at this point. Yesterday Benji was suspended, Sam had spent lunch alone in the library, and for the first time in history, James walked into the music room with Audrey Zhao.

"Marino's gone nuts. Seriously!" Jett leaned his head back, pouring a stream of soda down his throat. "What do you think?" He took a bite of his apple, and juice splattered across Chloe's face. She clenched her eyes shut, wiping herself with the sleeve of her sweater.

"I don't know."

"You don't think it was me," Jett said, setting his apple on the table, "do you?"

Chloe shook her head. "Of course not."

"Who do you think it could be, then?" He chuckled. "As much as I like to believe it's Noah, we all know he wouldn't have the guts. His throws are too weak to penetrate glass, anyway. Even Coach knows I'm superior, not that I did it."

Chloe bit her lip. "I mean, it could be an adult, right?"

"Seriously? The baseballs were from our school. It has to be someone from the team." He leaned his chin back to stare at the ceiling. "Or I guess it could be someone in softball, too. What girl on your team's got the best arm?"

Chloe's heart raced. She felt the hefty weight of the baseballs in her hand. Heard the shattering glass. Smelled the sour aroma of evergreens as the wind rattled through tree branches, whooshing past her. A tap on her shoulder saved her from the haunting memory. "Hey," someone said. "Let's talk."

"Well look who it is!" Jett chuckled, amused with himself. "Little Miss Perkins. Missing your maniac boyfriend already?"

Sam crossed her arms. "You never shut up, do you?"

"Talk about what?" Chloe asked. It felt like ages since the last time she spoke to Sam. The real Sam. The Sam who wasn't living inside the reclusive world of music. The Sam who spoke first. The Sam who always had something to complain about.

"Just come with me." She motioned for Chloe to follow, and the tension brewing between them dissolved. Chloe didn't bother giving Jett a goodbye. Not even a glance. She swept her food into her backpack and ran after Sam, who was already halfway to the door.

Samantha Perkins was back.

Leaning against the hallways lockers, they shared a common stillness. It was the first time they'd done so. Sam didn't complain about Audrey. She didn't hum to keep her thoughts from running. In exchange, Chloe didn't move. She didn't play with her hair. Didn't fill the air with valueless jokes Sam wasn't in the mood for.

Sam broke the silence. "I talked to Benji yesterday."

"What?" Chloe squinted at the hallway floors.

"I need you to meet us at Blueberry tonight. Six-thirty."

Chloe held her breath. After she finally accepted that fact that everyone would move on, an opportunity like this gets handed to her? Right as she gives up, everyone else takes action?

"He has something to tell us." Sam cleared her throat. "I have a feeling it's important."

Chloe felt an urge to hop between her feet and relieve the pressure from standing so long, but she resisted, trying to recall the last time all four of them were together at Blueberry. It was before Nina died—that was all she knew. No matter how intently she focused, the memory never came back. Although she was thrilled to experience that lost memory once again, the thought of facing Benji after what she'd done was too heavy to swallow. She shook her head slowly, still watching her boots. "I can't."

"Chloe—"

"Sorry, but I can't understand him. I think James was right—it's time we all move on from this madness and make some new friends." She unglued her feet from the floor, heading back to the cafeteria, but Sam stopped her by the fabric of her backpack.

"Seriously?" Sam laughed in half-humor, half mockery. "That's it? Come on, Chloe. At least give Benji a chance."

Chloe waited for Sam to release her backpack before turning around. "This doesn't have anything to do with him." Under the dim hallway lights, a dash of emerald melted through her eyes. "Nevermind, I—I'll be there."

Sam nodded as Chloe walked away. "Thank you."

Chloe opened the door to the cafeteria and paused. "Good luck with James."

CHAPTER 28

trapped

The afternoon of May 23rd. Benji's second day of suspension, and he had spent the entirety of it rehearsing the story of Nina. His future relied on explaining it perfectly, in a way where his friends wouldn't blast him with anger or trip his feet with questions. So he sat at his bedroom desk, the lights glowing dimly, his pen sweeping across the page. No matter how many times he crumpled them to restart, his smile never left.

He shut his eyes and imagined himself standing with his friends at the shore. He slipped away from them, unnoticed, watching with pride as he backed away into the fog. After a sweet walk to Candy Road and a shy wave at the town's weak lights, he was gone.

"Goodbye, Wishville." He leaned back in his chair, blinding himself with the ceiling light. The words tasted beautiful on his tongue. After tonight, he'd leave peacefully. He'd leave, and this time he'd be ready to disappear.

As he continued writing his explanation, he maintained the vision in his mind—the beautiful image of fading away after solving the puzzle he'd made. His pen froze when he glanced at the clock, a subtle reminder that today, time controlled him. It was four thirty. He'd have to leave soon, and his window would be the way out.

A car engine extinguished in the driveway. His pen wrote faster.

I need to leave the house at six. He nodded. *I'll make sure Mom sees me a few minutes before I leave, that way she won't check on me for a while.* The plan was simple. By the next time Rebecca searched his room, it'd be too late. He'd be exiting town.

A delicate tap traveled from the door. Leaving his pen and papers behind, Benji grabbed a book from the edge of his desk and hopped onto his bed. According to Mr. Trenton, he'd have to finish it by Monday, but this was the first time he'd touched it. He scrambled to a random page as the door swung open.

"I sent Lauren home." Rebecca peeked through the crack before sliding in. "What are you up to?" Her neck shifted in the direction of the pages on his desk, and Benji was hasty to bring her attention to something else.

"Thought I'd catch up on the reading." He lifted the book in his hands a little too energetically.

"You sure you're feeling okay?" As she made her way toward him, his instincts tugged at his spine, begging him to move as though Rebecca were pure poison. He forced himself to stay planted. Any strange behavior could soil his plans.

At first Benji thought Rebecca leaned to hug him, but her arms lay limp by her sides as she spouted a rehearsed statement. "Last time you met with Dr. Atkins you seemed to be in a much better mood." A piece of hair fell in front of her eyes, and she tucked it behind her ear with a gulp. "I booked another appointment with her for later today."

The book hopped between his fingertips before splatting onto the floor. "What do you mean, *today?*" Although Rebecca wasn't touching him, Benji may as well have been prying her fingers off his arm. "No." Benji rubbed his sore forehead. "No, that won't work. You can reschedule it, can't you?"

Rebecca fixed her posture, leaning away from him.

Calm, Benji. Think.

He reached over the edge of his bed to retrieve the book and reopened it. "You were right—I'm really not feeling well. Was planning to stay home and catch up on homework." There was not one tense muscle in his arms, but his mind was screaming. "Do you think she'd mind if we rescheduled?"

Rebecca stepped back, the distance between them swelling. "The meeting's at seven. You can relax until then."

"Seven?" The slipped urgency in his own voice made him cringe. "How about tomorrow?"

"You're going today." She walked backward to the doorway, and she swerved into the hallway, her arms stiffened. "Brought some sandwiches from the deli," she called through the hall. "Come eat."

Benji's last day alive. His last chance to leave. Although he wished the clocks would slow, the reality was that he had no time to waste. The hands clicked closer to 11:59. Closer to when he was scheduled to die.

"Mom?"

Rebecca sank her teeth into her sandwich as Benji

appeared in the dining room. She faced him with wide eyes and turkey protruding between her cracked lips.

"I'm gonna take a walk. I'll be back in time for the appointment." No matter how softly he set his feet on the floor, they shook the house with every step. The weight of his lie concentrated within his bones. He would not come back today.

He would never come back.

A hand squeezed his shoulder. "You're not going anywhere." Rebecca spun him around and swallowed her bite of meat. "Eat some food. You'll feel better."

Benji yanked his shoulder away from her. "I'm going." His voice was sterner than hers. At first Rebecca's teeth parted in disgust, but as soon as Benji had opened the door, they shut stronger than before. She reached past his head, slammed the door shut in his face. and waved her way in front of him. "Sit down." With a haunting snap, she locked the door behind her.

"Mom?" He searched her eyes, trying to find her.

"Sit."

"You don't understand." His eyes stung. "Today's not a good day for me."

She leaned her head back against the door, her lips shaking. "I know about your calendar." Her eyelids fell. "I know all of it."

Benji frowned. "Calendar?"

"Why was today circled in red?" Her voice vibrated through the floor.

Benji tried to remain calm, but his hot and sweaty palms distracted him.

"Tell me what happened." She brought a hand to her

forehead in hopes of suppressing her explosive thoughts. "Is someone bullying you? Making fun of your height?"

"No one's bullying me!" When he shouted, it sounded as if he were about to cry. He didn't mean for it to be that way. But it happened, and he was embarrassed of it, so he faced the ground with a sigh.

"Is this about your father? Please talk to me."

Benji refused to raise his chin. Eventually, her hand dropped from her head, and the waves in her forehead loosened. "What is it you can tell Dr. Atkins and not me?"

She cracked.

"You can talk to me." She gasped for breath, nearly drowning between words. "You can always talk to me. I'm your mom." Tears rolling over her cheek, she reached over and adjusting his face until he was looking at her. Benji's eyes, however, wandered away with their own will. "Tell me what happened."

Benji was slipping. His plan to bring everyone together—it grew increasingly ridiculous by the moment. So ridiculous that he doubted his own thoughts. *Am I really crazy? What if Dr. Atkins is right about Nina?* The next question hit him like a bullet to the chest.

Am I even going to die?

The room filled with ice. His sneakers on the dining room tile sent chills through his ankles. Each breath blurred his eyesight until he was blind. The room nothing more but a black hole. That's when the thoughts came. Thoughts he never thought he'd have. *What if no one believes me?* He threw his face into cupped hands. *What if they don't even come to Blueberry? What if I've messed up my life for no reason at all?*

He leaned into her, tightening his hands around her back. For a moment they stood together in the same place. Alone, lost in the dark. Their shared presence was enough to warm the room and fill it with light. But as Benji's vision trickled back to him, the gray room filled his eyes, and the light no longer appealed to him. He wanted to go back, but the air returned to it's normal chill, and Rebecca pulled herself away with arms stiffer than before.

"If you won't talk to me, you won't leave this room." She checked her watch. "You're going to sit down, eat your sandwich, and wait with me until your appointment. We'll go together, and maybe after we can grab some ice cream."

Silence.

She wiped away the remnants of her tears. "How does that sound?"

There was nothing to do except wait for an escape opportunity like a prisoner. He sat at the table, Rebecca watching him as he choked down what he knew would be his last meal. When he finished the sandwich, he didn't move. His mother's eyes on him and his own eyes on the dining room clock, Benji remembered the fun times he had with everyone—their countless meetings at Blueberry, playing tag and hide-and-seek, sneaking out while Lauren pretended to babysit him—and used these memories to stay strong. Today was a fist-fight with the odds against his favor. If he struck too early or too late he'd get beaten to death, but if he waited for the right moment, he might make it out alive.

The perfect timing to escape would be as they headed to the car, but he'd have to wait until they left for the appointment to do so. Rebecca wouldn't leave any earlier than six-thirty, the time he planned to meet everyone at Blueberry. Today, he'd have to trust that his friends would wait for him, but even if they did, he knew they wouldn't wait long. He had to get to Blueberry, and fast.

Benji assumed staring at the clock would slow time and allow him to further develop his plan, but the opposite was true. In a matter of seconds it was six thirty-five, and a knock came from the front door. Rebecca rubbed her damp cheek against her sleeve and stood.

When the door swung open, Benji lost his only opening for attack.

"I thought I'd drive you to your appointment." Mayor Perkins turned to Rebecca with a grin. "Shall we take your car or mine?"

CHAPTER 29

pedal

It was the longest car ride of his lifetime. Every detail through the window soaked into his brain. No filtering. Simply hopping right through his ears. He remembered the most minute details, like how many trees were on each block, and the color of every house that bordered the sidewalks, colors he hadn't noticed before.

As they drove down Main Street, he spotted Ms. Camille's flower shop, Seaside Cafe, and Chowdies, the place that crafted the chowder that flocked his childhood memories. With permission from Rebecca, Benji rolled the windows and welcomed a wild gust of salty air. He leaned back in his seat and allowed his sleep deprivation to capture him, shifting into a deep sleep. He lost track of time. For the first time this week, everything moved at a steady pace.

He rose Mayor Perkin's warm hands nudging his arm. "What time is it?" Benji jolted his head from the back of his seat, searching the sky for clues of how long he'd sleep.

"Don't worry." The mayor smiled. "We're not late."

In the passenger seat, Rebecca grabbed her purse and

left her car, waiting for Benji and Mayor Perkins to follow her. Benji saw his next opening as Mayor Perkins held the door open for him. Wishville had all kinds of hiding places in the forest—he remembered from his games of hide-and-seek in elementary school. He could leave right now and hide until he had a chance to get to Candy Road unnoticed. This was it.

As soon as Benji's head caught the first glimpse of day, Mayor Perkins wrapped a tight arm around his shoulder and led him in the direction of the building.

That's when it dawned on him—they both knew he had something planned. They had it all wrong, but there was no way for Benji to explain the truth, not when there was no time left. He needed to get to Blueberry before he lost his chance.

There was only one hurdle left in his life. One last thing to overcome. One last challenge. And with time approaching seven, he had five hours to pursue it.

The first step was to get out of this appointment.

He knew how long these sessions could take. His last meeting with Dr. Atkins lasted about half an hour. At that rate, everyone would have left Blueberry and gone home with him completely forgotten. If he wanted to get there faster, he'd need a plan to cut it short.

When Mayor Perkins guided him through the office door, Benji knew escaping would be no easy task. The only exit was through the door he had entered from, which led to the waiting room, where Mayor Perkins and Rebecca acted as guards. That meant he had one option left.

The window.

"Please, have a seat." Dr. Atkins gestured to the sofa

and sat herself comfortably across from him. "It's been a while. How are you feeling today?"

If I run from here to Blueberry, I could get there in less than ten minutes. Benji's heart beat faster. *But I'd have to leave right now.*

"Is there something on your mind?" Dr. Atkins asked.

"Oh no, nothing really." Benji laughed, his brows slightly furrowed. "I'm stressing a little about this presentation tomorrow."

"I was told you've been suspended."

"Did I say tomorrow?" He pinned his focus on the window. "I meant in two weeks. When I get back."

"I see. What subject?"

"Math."

She tilted her head. "I don't believe I've ever heard of a presentation in math class before."

"My school, you know . . ." Benji grinned at the shimmering glass. "Very creative teachers."

He caught her smiling through the corner of his eye. *I'm running out of time.* Benji gulped. *I need to think of something fast. Now.*

Dr. Atkins cleared her throat. "I'd like to—"

"Actually, I have a question for *you*, Dr. Atkins." Benji pulled his focus from the window, staring her straight in the eyes. "Do you ever notice the colors?"

"Colors?"

"When I walk into a room, the first thing I do is look at the colors of the wall. My wall at home is a light gray, the school hallway is beige—you can tell if you look at the strip of open space above the lockers—and the inside of Chowdies is white. But not pure white. More of an eggshell color."

"The colors interest you?"

"But I can't remember the color of the waiting room." He grabbed his head. "I can't remember. I wasn't paying attention."

"It's white, I believe."

"But what kind?" He gripped his head harder, fingers tense. "Cream? Blue tone?"

She hummed to herself. "Actually, I'm not too—"

"Can you check for me, please?" Benji's hands fell from his head, lying dead on his lap. He shook his head at the floor, eyes shut. "I have to know. If I don't know, then I'm not sure—"

"How about after we talk, we can go check the wall together. Does that sound nice?"

He searched the room for a clock. Nothing. *I have no other choice.* He noticed a floor lamp standing boldly beside the sofa, and the tips of his lips curved into a slight grin.

"No!" He folded his fingers together in his lap and tucked his chin into his chest. "I need to know the color. I need to know." He stood, breathing heavily, and took a step toward her. "I need to know."

Although Dr. Atkins held still, calm and controlled, Benji was positive he saw her lips flinch. "Would you like to check now and come back?" Her voice was soft, but it held a twinge of urgency.

"I need to know!" Benji stomped a foot on the floor, letting a whine leave his mouth. "Check! I need to know. I need to—"

Dr. Atkins stood with wide eyes. "I'll peek in the room for you."

Benji paused his fit to nod. A grin struck his lips against control, but luckily, Dr. Atkins already had her back to him. With soft steps, Benji approached the edge of the sofa and wrapped his fingers around the cold stem of the lamp. As soon as Dr. Atkins set her hand on the knob, he rotated the lamp sideways and stormed for the window.

"What are you—" She jolted around, leaving the half-open door behind her.

Glass shattered across the floor. Benji struck the base of the rod against the surviving pieces until he'd blasted enough space to jump through. Before Dr. Atkins could reach him, he gripped the windowsill and propelled himself outside without hesitation.

His feet burned at impact, and his knees ached as he stood. Luckily, the jump was not more than a few feet. There wasn't enough time to think. He had to keep moving.

"What happened?" Rebecca's shout echoed from inside.

"I—well—" Dr. Atkins voice was shakier than he'd ever heard it before.

Run.

Benji dashed down the road as fast as he could, hoping to leave before they noticed which direction he traveled in. However, when he looked over his shoulder, Dr. Atkins's head peeked out of the shattered window.

"Shoot." He ran faster.

Jett cruised around the corner on his bike when he

saw Benji running full speed, shards of glass linking to his shirt and his right arm covered in cuts. "What the—"

Benji stumbled to a stop in front of him. "Get off your bike." He was panting.

"Benji?" Jett's face twisted into a pretzel. "What are you—"

Benji reached for him with his bloody arm. "Just get off already!"

Jett leaned away from him with disgust, but when he heard shouting from Dr. Atkins' office, he was quick to hop off. He backed away as Benji got on, nearly tripping over his own legs. He hadn't ridden a bike since James let him borrow his in fourth grade. The pedals were difficult to reach, but he managed to get the bike to function by stretching his toes as far as possible. "Thanks." And Benji was off, leaving the befuddled Jett to deal with explaining himself to the mayor and a stunned psychologist.

Wheel skid behind him as Benji turned the corner. Rebecca's face was glued to Mayor Perkins' passenger seat window, watching him with a blank face. Before they could make a move, Benji steered a sharp right and shot his way through a thick layer of trees. The perfect place to escape a chasing car. The cuts on his arm stung as the wind rushed past him, but he was too focused on balancing to notice. He couldn't fall. That'd waste too much time, but he also couldn't risk biking too slow. He took the risk and pedaled faster.

His legs were jello as he navigated the clumps of trees and bushes approaching. He made so many twists he nearly forgot where he was headed. Emerging from the clumps of trees onto a neighborhood sidewalk, the image of Blueberry flashed in his mind. He narrowed his eyes, zooming past rows of identical gray homes

Benji spotted Mr. Trenton walking his dog at the far end of the sidewalk. "What time is it?" Benji called, pedaling toward him.

Mr. Trenton lifted his wrist. "Ten after seven." As Benji passed him, his smile disappeared. "Why are you bleed—"

"Thanks, Mr. Trenton." Benji laughed, nearly losing balance. "You're my favorite teacher." He turned at the corner, escaping from Mr. Trenton's line of sight, and swerved into a familiar group of trees off the side of the road. He couldn't risk traveling anywhere he'd be seen, or he'd be tracked down. Even if it took longer, he'd travel along the outskirts of Wishville, hiding among the evergreens.

As he traveled on his dirt path to Blueberry, a droplet of rain landed on the roof of his head. The gray clouds darkened, and the wind blew faster, ruffling tree branches and sweeping away excess dirt in clumps of brown fog. Although Benji couldn't remember the last time it rained in Wishville, his only concern was biking as fast as he could. He coughed the musty air out of his lungs and pedaled on, legs cursed with fatigue.

I'll make it.

CHAPTER 30

hero

James ran his fingers along the empty shelves of his bedroom. The only books that remained were a few textbooks he'd brought from school to spend time doing extra studying on. The material was far too easy for him, but he drilled through extra practice assignments anyway. Normally when he was tired of studying he'd work on solving a wooden puzzle, but now he simply paced around the room, running his hands on the different shelves and washing the dust off before going back to his textbooks.

It was 7:36. James was supposed to be at Blueberry an hour ago, but he couldn't bring himself to leave his room. The thought of seeing everyone together made him sick. All the pain he put himself through to reach progress would lose their value. He wouldn't be weak anymore. He'd resist.

When he finished running his fingers along the final shelf, he raised his hand and frowned at the dust accumulating on his palm. No matter how many times a day he walked around the room, dragging his hands where his books and puzzles used to be, there was always dust.

Small pieces of himself that he could never get rid of, and they made him sick.

He left his room to wash his hands. As he passed the stairs, a group of three rushed into the house. Rebecca, the Mayor, and Chloe's sister. They spoke over each other, explaining the situation to Mr. Koi in a wave of useless words. James stopped at the stairs, peering at the scene like a seagull watches its prey from above. Waiting for an entrance.

Mr. Koi held a hand in the air, silencing the room. "They're missing?"

Chloe's sister covered her face with open palms, and Rebecca wrapped an arm around her.

"At first it was only Benji. Rebecca and I went to my place to find out if Sam knew anything, but she wasn't there. Chloe hasn't been home either. We're guessing the three of them are together."

Mr. Koi cleared his throat. "Come down here."

Even without eye contact, James knew his father was speaking to him. He walked down the steps, the other adults finally noticing his presence. They waited until he reached the final step before shooting him with questions.

"Have you spoken to Benji in the last few days?"

"Has Chloe been acting weird to you lately?"

"Why would Sam go with them?"

James held his head firm. His answer was instantaneous. "I don't know anything."

The room silenced. Chloe's sister turned away, hiding her tears, and Rebecca crossed her arms to conceal their stiffness. Mayor Perkins, however, stood proud with his calmness at a steady peak. "Look, we don't know the entire story, but this could be a dangerous situation." He leaned forward, hovering over James. "So tell me again. Do you know something about this, or do you not?"

James blinked.

"We don't know what type of danger Benji might bring to the others. He's going through a lot right now." Mayor Perkins placed an arm on his shoulder, pressing James into the ground. "If you care about your friends, you'll tell us what you know."

Calling Benji dangerous should've been a ridiculous assumption. A few months ago the thought of it would make an entire room laugh. Benji may have been reckless and over-curious at times, but in terms of danger, that floppy-haired shortie was capable of nothing more than littering a candy wrapper. But now, as James stood analyzing the situation, the realization layered over him. Benji was planning something—he gathered that much from Sam—and whatever it was, he intended on dragging the others into it. Benji had always been the type to act alone. What was with sudden change of heart?

"Do you want to help your friends or not?" Mayor Perkins pulled his hand away. "What if they're planning to leave, huh? You're just gonna stand by and let them wander to their death?"

Normally, words came naturally to James in times of need. He'd be calm. Focused. But right now, his mind was scattered.

James stared at his toes. *What to do?* he asked himself. *Oh, what to do? What do I—*

Mr. Koi rushed over and raised James's chin with a

quick jolt of his hand. "Speak the truth." His voice was soft, but threatening.

James tried to jerk himself away. This time, Mr. Koi grabbed him by the shoulders and stared deep into his eyes. "Just say it, James!" It was the first time he heard him shout in what felt like years. His temper wasn't easy to coax out of hiding, and as crazy as it sounds, James was afraid.

"I—I don't—"

The adults formed a circle around him. Mr. Koi's grip tightened, and James found it hard to breath. Claustrophobic. The air shrunk around him.

"I know where they are." James yanked his eyes from his father, observing his shoes. "The forest up north. There's an old shed."

Mr. Koi pushed James away, turning to Mayor Perkins with a deep sigh of relief.

"Howell's old place." Mayor Perkins grabbed his jacket from the couch and headed for the door. "I'll find them."

"Please," Rebecca said softly. "Please, save my son."

"I will." Mayor Perkins set his hand on the doorknob and paused. "I'll do what's necessary." There was a firm nod, and he was gone.

As the front door swung desperately in the wind, James's blood boiled, but this time, he didn't question it.

"You did well." Mr. Koi reached to wrap his frozen arm around him, but James stepped out of the way and raced upstairs.

The empty shelves once filled with books haunted him. The desk once cluttered with wooden puzzles was now barren, his math and science textbooks sitting lonely on the top. His bed was thrown together care-lessly, bedsheets overlapping in uneven patterns. And when he looked in the mirror, a stranger looked back.

CHAPTER 31

question

Benji rolled Jett's bike into the nearest bush. Although his plan was to burst inside Blueberry, he paused at the mossy door. What if no one was inside? What if they hadn't waited for him, or hadn't come in the first place? He shook his head. Now was not the right time to be afraid.

When Benji opened the door, Sam leaned against the opposite wall, eyes narrowed and arms crossed. "You're late."

Benji shut the door behind him, relief rushing through his veins. He shut his eyes briefly, refreshing the spark that he'd dulled over time. *I can do this.*

Sam sat on the rug next to Chloe, who picked at her boot buckles with a vacant mind. Benji searched the rest of the room.

Empty.

"Look . . ." Sam pulled the fringes of the rug as if trying to yank its organs out. "I know what I told you, but I wasn't able to get James to come. I went to his house after school to tell him to meet us here and he—you know—didn't."

Benji sat, joining them.

"I tried," Sam said. "Promise."

It wasn't disappointment Benji felt. He knew that whether James was here or not, he still had people willing to listen, but when he raised his chin to speak, the ice in his throat prevented him from doing so. Where could he begin? He had memorized his story word for word, but now that he sat with them, he blanked. Their knowledge-thirsty eyes froze him solid.

Chloe stopped playing with her boots. "What happened to your arms?" She pointed to the fresh cuts, and Benji glued his arms to his sides in hopes of concealing them. What could he say? Tell them he broke through Dr. Atkins' window before stealing Jett's bike?

"I fell."

Sam pursed her lips, unconvinced, but Benji didn't give her the chance to ask any questions. "I really don't have much time, so I'll try to explain this fast." The words flowed once again, his warm formula of belief returning. He explained how Nina had predicted her own death that day in the hospital. How Oliver was the only man who could help Benji understand what he needed to do. Why he blew up when Jett vandalized Oliver's property. He mentioned the meeting with the psychologist, who had a red envelope from Nina, and how that same day, he had attempted to leave town once again, but failed. And when he finished explaining everything, only one question lingered in the air.

"But *why*?" Sam asked. "Why'd you care whether or not Nina could tell the future?"

"It doesn't really matter in the end, anyway." Chloe tossed her legs out in front of her and took down her ponytail. "To think you even went to Stricket for help, of all people. It doesn't make any sense."

The eyes watched him. He longed to keep the last piece of the puzzle hidden, but decided it wouldn't be fair. If either of them were in his shoes, he'd want the full story. So after a long breath, Benji willed himself to let the final secret leave him.

"I cared," he said, "because on that same day, she also gave me an envelope with the exact date and time of *my* death."

The room froze.

Chloe stopped twirling her hair. "And . . . you opened it?" The same question they all asked.

"Yeah." Benji nodded. "Sam, that night you gave me away. My mom didn't believe me. I was angry, the envelope was there, and I—"

"What do you mean Sam gave you away?" Chloe asked.

"So I opened it, and I . . ."

Sam's face went red. "Wait, so you're telling me this is my fault?"

"No, not at all. I . . ." Benji sighed. "Listen, I'm sorry for all the mess I've created. I've been distracted. So when you get the chance, please tell James that I'm sorry for not being there for him. For being so insensitive. I was in my own world."

"Why don't you just tell him yourself?" Chloe asked. "You could . . ."

The sound of a roaring engine interrupted her. She stood from the rug and peeked through Blueberry's door, searching for the origin of the strange noise. Benji traced his fingers along the grooves of his watch, trying to calm himself down.

It didn't work.

"A car." Chloe locked the front door. It was an old, weak door, but it'd have to keep them safe for now. "But why would—"

"Did you see who it was?" Sam stood, and Benji followed.

"It's . . ." Chloe ran her fingers through her tangled hair. "It's the mayor."

Benji leaned over, his breaths tightening by the second.

"Hey," Sam said, "what's going on?"

There was no time for a response, not that he'd be able to give one. A car door slammed from outside. Any moment now and Mayor Perkins would burst into the room.

Benji headed to the back door. "I need to leave."

Chloe slid in front of him, blocking his path. "Why are you running from him?" Her voice was serious, a tone none had heard from her before.

Benji attempted to shoot around her. "I don't have time to explain."

Chloe stepped in front of him again. "What else are you hiding from us?"

Footsteps echoed from the deck.

"Well?" Chloe turned to Sam, who stood watching blankly. "What do we do?"

"If what Benji said is true," Sam said, "then maybe we should let him go."

"What if he's trying to leave town again?" Chloe's eyes exploded with copper flames. "If he really told us the truth, then why'd he lie about his arm being cut up? Why would the mayor be looking for us? Are they looking for *you*? Did you do something? Because if you did then I—"

The pounding footsteps from the deck began to shake the building. Benji was beginning to sweat. "Sorry, I gotta go."

Chloe looked between the door and Benji. Sam caught her eye, and in that moment, the confusion washed from Chloe's face. She grabbed Benji by the shoulders and shoved him in the direction of the door. "Mayor Perkins!" She shouted louder. "Mayor! Benji's—"

"You idiot!" Sam kicked Chloe in the shin and watched her jump away. "You obviously don't know Benji."

Chloe leaned against the wall with a wince, and the fire in her eyes dampened to a coal. She stood empty against the wall, not an ounce of soul left in her. Benji couldn't decipher her response, but he had no time to piece together another puzzle. Pounding came from the door. "Chloe, is that you?" More pounding. "Open up!" The voice was warm and bold—the voice of the mayor.

Chloe groggily limped her way to the door. Her presence was dead, vacant, like a living ghost. She pushed her entire body weight into each step, and the floorboards creaked under her violently. The mayor shouted from the other side of the door as he fidgeted with the handle. Chloe reached for the lock.

Benji stepped toward her. "Chloe, don't—"

No time. Sam swung the back door open and tossed Benji through it. "Hurry!"

She shut the door silently behind them as the front burst open and footsteps trailed in. Chloe's soft voice babbled about her side of the story. Benji and Sam both knew that Mayor Perkins would come pouncing out the back at any second.

Adrenaline rushed through him. Benji stepped toward the safety of trees, escape the only thought in mind, but Sam caught him by the shoulder.

"I have one last question for you."

When he spun around, two watery eyes gazed into his mind.

"What day did Nina say you'd die?"

Benji leaned forward and wrapped his tattered arms around her. "I think you already know the answer."

By the time Mayor Perkins and Chloe opened the back door, Sam was alone.

CHAPTER 32

help

Puddles appeared every few steps, and Benji didn't have time to dodge them. He ran through, mud seeping through socks, splashes drenching his jeans. His calves burned with each step.

Continuing on this path through the forest was only a plea to be found. *I need to get out of here.* Benji turned. His arms stung as drops of rain smacked against them, but he kept running. For a while he was trapped in a daze. Not knowing where he was going—or why he made certain twists between trees, changing directions—but when he saw an old house in front of him, he woke up.

He hadn't come this way on purpose, yet at the same time, it was genius. If he wanted to avoid getting caught, he'd need to stay far from the main parts of town. The last place they'd look was Eudora Hill. As long as Chloe didn't tell anyone, no one would discover his relationship to Oliver.

Benji ran faster, and the shower accelerated, mirroring him. How long had it been since the last time it rained in Wishville? The memory was lost in his mind.

He arrived at the steps of Oliver's home. The house had changed from the last time he saw it, and it made him sick. The place was patched like old jeans, each broken window covered in boards. The image of Oliver slamming the door in his face shot through him, along with the memory of his argument with Jett. Benji had an urge to step away, but instead of acknowledging it, he confronted the steps and knocked on the door.

All he could hear was the pummeling rain on the wooden deck and flowing from the overhang above him.

Drip. A single droplet trickled from the overhand onto his shoe, a second following his head. He knocked again.

A buzz struck the deck, and although he wasn't fully sure if Oliver's footsteps or the wind was the cause, he clung to optimism, pounding harder.

"Oliver!" He knocked until his knuckles went red. "Oliver!"

The door slammed open violently, and the old man stood in front of him with a dead look in his eyes.

Benji turned to the deck floor. *What am I doing here, anyway?* A twist formed in his stomach. How could this day have possibly gone wrong? Why did Benji have to drag so many people into his own mess? It was his fault. All of it. If he had only contained his emotions and controlled himself. If he had remained silent after Nina died. If he had never opened the envelope. If he had used his brain correctly, none of this would have happened!

"I'm sorry." Benji bit his shivering lip and stepped away, but Oliver stopped him with a hand on his shoulder.

"It's tonight, isn't it?" His voice was softer than usual.

Benji nodded, and Oliver released his shoulder before disappearing into the broken home.

This time, the door was left open for him.

With a towel around his shoulders, Benji waited in the living room for Oliver. The house was silent, and although he appreciated the slow pace, something about it made him tense. He observed the room carefully, soaking in every last detail.

Oliver emerged from the kitchen with a red cup and slipped it into Benji's hands. "Hot chocolate." The mug was warm.

Before he could take a sip, Oliver pulled at his ear, leading Benji to nearly spill the hot drink over himself. "Just kidding."

Coffee. A smile appeared every time he brought the mug to his lips, fading when pulled away. Lauren was the only person to use that trick. The thought of coffee in the square initiated a flow of memories. The town festivals, although dreaded, would never be forgotten. The cold ocean and pesky seagulls would never cease to haunt him. His memories with everyone—the fun talks at Blueberry, dinner at the Kois' house, and eating lunch at their favorite cafeteria table. The memories were sweet in his mind, yet also bitter. Like coffee.

There were no instructions. No demands. Oliver sprawled back on the couch and propped his feet onto the table. He sipped on his own drink. Benji joined him, even leaning his back against the couch cushion as though he'd be relaxing there for hours. It was almost a normal night.

A minute could've passed, but it felt like an hour. When Benji's cup was empty, he set it on the table and straightened his back. "I don't know where to start."

Oliver waited.

"I'm guessing you haven't heard about the fights? My suspension? How I sorta blasted through a window?"

He chuckled. "Eudora isn't a popular spot for gossip."

"I had a plan tonight." He raised his chin, but still avoided eye contact. "You know, to bring everyone together."

"I'm guessing it didn't end well?"

Benji turned his cheek, ready to look Oliver in the eye, but the man was staring at his lap. When he finally looked up, he was smiling. "You did your best."

Benji shook from the thought of leaving, and Oliver wrapped an arm around him for stability. Instantly, Benji's trembling vanished, and his brain thawed. "To think I'll die." Benji shook his head. "The last thing I wanted to accomplish before leaving, and I failed." A moment flew by. Or maybe a few. "What will I do?"

"It's simple. You'll stay here tonight." Oliver set his mug on the floor, hopped to his feet, and planted his boot on a stack of books by the wall. He reached for a clock on the wall, his voice unsteady as he tried to remain balanced on the choppy stack. "I'll stop all the clocks and—"

"I can't." Benji stood, pacing through the room. The

pieces were falling together again. "I wouldn't let myself leave town before because I hadn't completed my goal." The spark in his eyes rekindled itself. "And I still haven't. But that doesn't mean—"

"Benji." Oliver stepped down from the books, tossing an analog clock onto the coffee table. "You need to calm down." His breath staggered from the task, as if taking down a clock was more tiresome than running a mile. "We don't know anything for sure. It's safer for you to stay here in case the unexpected happens. We don't know if—"

"There's no reason to stay. This whole time I've been trying to leave behind some kind of legacy. I thought that if I completed a bunch of random tasks, I'd finally let myself leave. But that's not it. I just had to be ready to let this all go." Benji paused in the center of the room, his gray eyes locked on Oliver. "And I've never felt more ready than I do right now."

Oliver's face hardened. "Any sane man wouldn't let you go."

Benji wasn't in the mood for running again, but it seemed his body had prepared itself for the task. His legs went tense, and he pointed himself in the direction of the door.

The man was too fast. Oliver snatched his wrist, and Benji jumped toward the door, hoping to pull himself free. There was no time to shout.

"Luckily," Oliver tightened an object to him, nearly choking Benji's wrist, "I'm not sane." He released him with a violent thrust toward the wall, grinning widely.

Benji raised his burning wrist in front of him.

Contrasting the cuts on his right arm was a handsome silver watch.

"You're not leaving without a way to keep track of time." Oliver's eyes glowed. There was something new in his eyes today. Something foreign.

Benji opened his mouth to thank him, but the words wouldn't flow.

By the time the car reached the base of Eudora Hill, it was already 11:39. With less than twenty minutes left, Oliver slammed his foot on the pedal. He drove along the outskirts of town at a dangerous speed, but he still managed to speak calmly. "Are you sure you wanna do this?"

Benji gazed through the windshield.

"I can come with you." The words sounded bizarre coming from Oliver. "There's nothing left for me here, anyway."

Benji wasn't sure why the offer seemed so awful to him. Perhaps he wanted to accomplish his last goal before death alone. "This is on me, not you."

A raccoon sprinted across the winding road, and Oliver swerved the wheel in shock. Benji shut his eyes, heart pounding, his right arm throbbing. The car stopped with a screech, sideways on the winding road.

His heart still racing, Benji looked at Oliver in the driver's seat. The man's eyes glowed in the dark. "Stupid pests." He lifted his foot from the brakes, his grip on the wheel tighter than before.

As Benji neared his final destination, his stomach twisted inside of him. The rain pounding on the windshield coupled with the swerving of the car at blasting speeds nauseated him. The world spun out of control. His body ached. He could hardly move.

He was fading.

"Lean your head against the back," Oliver said.

He did. No help.

They reached Candy Road as the clock struck 11:45. Oliver pulled over at the bottom of the road, letting out a sigh of relief. "Need me to walk you?"

Benji peeked through the window at Candy Road, his head throbbing. So many trees. Through them were his final steps of his life. "I got it from here."

Oliver reached into the back seat and rummaged through some junk. A few moments later, he pulled out an umbrella as black as the night. He held it toward Benji as if it were a prized sword.

Benji took it from him with a grin before sliding outside the car door. This time, the words were able to leave his throat.

"Thank you."

The man said nothing in return. He stared at him with caramel eyes—eyes that held two precious stories behind them. Benji shut the door, knowing this was the last time he'd ever see him.

The car stood silent, letting the moment seep in. It drove away at a safe, steady speed, leaving Benji alone in his fast-paced race against time.

Benji was quick to move on. He opened the umbrella, held it over his head, and scaled the tree roots of Candy Road, checking his watch along the way.

11:47. Twelve minutes.

Benji didn't bother thinking anymore. He shoved the idea of death into the dark recess of his mind. From there it gnawed at the end of his brain, but he ignored the pain and focused instead on the trees that summoned him. They shook in the wind, dancing with the ticks of the clock.

Benji neared the top of Candy Road. He could see just above the bridge—the tips of trees that stood across the border. With a peek to the right, he spotted the lights of the square, as they always looked from above. Beautiful. He saw his elementary school sitting next to Wishville Junior High, as well at the high school next to it—the school he would never attend. Lastly, he raised his face eye-level with Oliver's home on Eudora Hill. In a few moments, Wishville would be nothing more than a tart memory.

"I'm ready." He shut his eyes as he reached the base of the bridge. "Goodbye, Wishville." The salty air filled his lungs for what he knew to be his final taste of town.

But when Benji opened his eyes, he wasn't alone.

CHAPTER 33

bridge

"Take a deep breath, and calm down." The man's voice was soothing, but eyes told another story. "Everything's going to be okay. You'll get in the car, I'll take you home, and this mess will finally be over."

Benji's eyes glowed under the light of the crescent moon, which hovered like a dragonfly over the ocean. He couldn't deny that he found Mayor Perkins' promise appealing. His car blocked the path out of town, lying crooked near the end of the bridge, shimmering in the moonlight. Benji imagined sitting in the front seat. On their way down Candy Road, the heater would blast through the vehicle, and he would finally be warm again. He'd fall asleep with his head leaned gently against the window, listening to the gentle trickling of rain against the glass. He could die there in comfort. He could end this.

Snap out of it!

Benji flung his umbrella to the side of the dirt road. As he stood at the bridge entrance, rain poured over him like sunshine at dusk, soaking his dry clothes for a second time. The waves roared, and for a moment, he almost smiled. "Move aside."

There was only one man and one car in front of him. A man who cared for Benji and cared for this town. A man he had known his entire life. But as he stared into his hollow eyes now, he wondered if Mayor Perkins had ever known *him*.

Then there was a car. A car that was his easy way out. A car that, in Benji's eyes, was a beautiful ending to his story. But as he stared at the bulky machinery, the realization hit that perhaps it was nothing more than a gas-powered facade.

The trees called Benji from the other side. He took a step forward, and they rustled, spouting his name. The waves hastened their speed, ordering him to move faster. He glanced at his new clock. It reflected the sparkling stars on his cheeks.

Ten minutes left.

"You're killing yourself, Benji." Mayor Perkins spoon-fed doubts into Benji's mind, hoping they might overcome whatever evil virus had overtaken him.

The night was cold. He could tell by the way Mayor Perkin's arms were crossed. Benji wasn't shaking, despite not having a sweatshirt on.

Mayor Perkins rubbed his arms and cleared his throat. "I have one question for you, and I expect you to answer it." His voice was piercing. Sharp. "Are you getting in the car or not?"

Benji wanted his answer to be easy. He wanted to shake his head, tell him to let him be, and run into the unknown. But thoughts clotted his mind and he couldn't think clearly anymore. It took all of his strength to choke out the word *no*, and as soon as he did, Mayor Perkins had resorted to his backup plan.

He reached behind his back, retrieving a gun that he held firmly in front of him. He spoke once more. "Get in the car."

Tick.

Time was slipping away. His destination was so close, yet so far, and he couldn't bring himself to step forward in fear that it might be his last step. *This isn't how it's supposed to go.*

Benji kept his eyes locked on the gun, thinking, but the shining metal blinded his thoughts.

"This town has suffered so much grief because of you." His eyes watered. "Now please, get in the car so I won't be forced to end this grief myself."

Benji's muscles locked.

Mayor Perkins stepped forward. "It doesn't have to end like this. Go on." He tightened his grip on the gun. "Get in the car."

Tock.

Benji's walked toward the car, slowly, his heart racing faster than he could think. The mayor loosened his sore fingers on the gun.

He touched the cold door handle, and at that moment, the town froze. Oliver's car paused on its way back to Eudora. Rebecca stopped searching through town. The mayor transformed into a statue. Everything and everyone in Wishville came to a halt, leaving Benji trapped in a broken world. The only noise he heard were a few distant footsteps. They were soft, hardly noticeable, but the voice that followed was urgent, infecting the air. "Let him go!"

Benji turned, keeping the mayor within his peripheral vision. On the opposite end of the bridge was someone he knew. A girl.

Sam.

She leaned over, hands on her knees, gasping for breath. With her appearance, the town unpaused, and everything set into motion again. The busy clocks ticked as Sam straightened her back. "Dad." Her breathing was steady now. "Put down the gun."

He flinched as though she'd appeared out of thin air. "Samantha?"

"Put down the gun!"

Mayor Perkins pulled his focus away from her, turning to Benji. "Get in the car."

Sam stormed toward him with eyes of fire. "Let him go."

The waves raced, clapping against themselves louder than thunder. The three of them breathed rapidly out of sync as the rain soaked their clothes. Sam's frizzy hair stuck to the sides of her cheeks like two flat papers. The waves were noisy, and Benji wished to mute them.

He waited for the sounds to settle in his mind before looking away from Sam, his eyes directed at the ground. "Go back home."

Backing away, Sam studied both Benji and the mayor in disbelief. She placed her shaky hands onto the railing of the bridge, and with a deep breath, hoisted the rest of her body onto the ledge. After straightening her legs, she held her arms out to balance herself.

Finally, Mayor Perkins peeled his focus off Benji. "Get down from there."

"Drop the gun."

He tightened his grip. "Get down this instant!"

"If you don't let Benji leave, I'll jump off. I'll do it."

"Samantha." There was a pinch of humor in his voice. The left side of his face stretched higher than the right, the tips of his lips gently curved. "Let's not play games, now."

Benji watched their conversation silently. It was happening too fast to understand. When he finally found the strength in him, he took a step away from the car door and allowed his fingers to fall from the handle. "Sam?" He thought he called her name, but the world was too loud to hear himself, so he wasn't fully sure.

Sam focused on her sneakers. "Let him go." Her eyes wandered to the hundreds of feet below, and she lost the little coordination she had in her legs. She leaned to the side, gathering her balance.

Mayor Perkin's face reddened. He brought the gun above his head and hurled it into the sea below. "There!" He faced Sam, breathing through gritted teeth. "You happy? Now come down."

Sam grinned at Benji, satisfied with her success, but he wasn't able to smile back. As she leaned forward to step off, the rain slipped its way under her shoes. Her arms swerved to gather balance once more, but by the time Benji had taken a single step, she had already disappeared.

The waves squirted mists of excitement through the night sky, eager for their next meal.

Tick.

Even now, Benji couldn't silence the ticking in the back of his head. He stood on the bridge, his head throbbing with each tock. The world was spinning.

The mayor didn't have time to shout. He rushed to the ledge, his arms no longer cold.

Benji didn't understand. There was no way. It wasn't possible.

Blank. His thoughts vanished.

The bridge was gray. A dark, menacing gray. The kind of gray that fills a room before and after death. The gray filled Benji's eyes, fading his vision into darkness. Before transitioning into a permanent black, the moonlight brightened his vision, shining a beam of light onto a pair of fumbling hands. They gripped tighter to the railing, and Sam's head and shoulders emerged from the misty air. With a final push, Sam propelled herself over the railing and tumbled onto the bridge pavement. She lay on the ground, shaking. Freezing.

Tock.

She sat up slowly. Scrapes covered her wrists and elbows. She had managed to catch herself by the bottom of the railing and drag herself up, but only with the exchange of blood. Despite the red blotches smeared on her arms, she stared blankly in front of her, unknown to the pain. Benji walked toward Sam with a weightless soul.

Mayor Perkins knelt by Sam's side and wrapped his trembling arms around her. "Samantha," he whispered.

"Sam," Benji echoed, taking another step forward.

"Get away from my daughter!" The back of Mayor Perkins' neck was so tense it left Benji petrified. "Go ahead and leave. Do it. I'm not stopping you."

Benji couldn't bring himself to move. "Sam." Rain streamed over his eyes, blurring his vision. "Say something, please!"

The color returned to her skin, and she pushed her father away from her. "You idiot." She smiled with dry lips, her eyes on Mayor Perkins, but Benji knew she was speaking to him. "Just run."

Benji shut his eyes and let the water roll over his face in a refreshing massage. A simple phrase, but he'd been longing to hear it his entire life. With a final breath of Wishville's sour air, he climbed over the hood of Mayor Perkins' car, jumped to the other side, and sprinted to the *LEAVING WISHVILLE* sign.

He reached the end of town.

And he kept going.

Running.

Ran.

CHAPTER 34

shine

The first step outside Wishville was not how Benji imagined it would be. He thought he'd be ten times lighter, and each of his footsteps would glide gently across the dirt. But as he ran from town into the unknown, his feet were heavy and slammed with each step. His breaths were dangerous, as if each wad of air was afraid it'd be the last.

The extension of Candy Road was nothing strange until it came to a curve. He followed through this unfamiliar twist, believing it would lead to a monster planning to eat him alive, or a forest fire ready to burn him. But all he saw was the same old road, leading to nothing but a blur of darkness in the distance.

Benji slowed and came to a stop. He peeked over his shoulder for the first time, yearning for a final glance of Wishville, but all he could see were trees.

Somewhere in town was his mom. All of his old friends. Sam was being eased into the car by Mayor Perkins. Chloe was probably explaining the crazy night to her sister, James under his covers without a book and a flashlight, and Jett wondering where his bike had ended up. For a moment, Benji felt as if the entire town had given up on him. They had all tried so hard to bring him back to normal, to bring him back to the kid he used to be before all the madness occurred. But then, in the middle of thought, Benji realized he had it backward.

He had given up on Wishville.

"And I really hope I made the right choice." He took a deep breath, raised his chin, and continued down the road, forcing himself through the blackness. *If I'm gonna die*, Benji thought. *I'll die as far from Wishville as possible.*

The rumble of darkness continued to move at the same steady pace he was running at. The trees all looked the same, and to Benji it felt as though he was going nowhere. It was only when he met a fork in the road that he received a feeling of progress. He took a left without debate, a soreness spreading through his legs. He had run too much today.

So he slowed down, noticing his glimmering watch. 11:54. Five minutes. He gulped.

Five minutes was the amount of time Mr. Trenton would give them for a short break during class. Benji remembered not doing much during those breaks. He might draw something, or maybe bother James by distracting him from his book. At those times, five minutes were so meaningless. But now he only had five minutes left to live. Five minutes until his last breath. He started to run again, the various possibilities of his death flashing through his mind. Maybe lightning would strike him from the dark clouds above, or a tree would crash down on his skull. Maybe a rabid animal would hop from a bush a few moments from now, licking its last meal off its lips. But what scared Benji the most was the uncertainty of it all. Goosebumps raised on his arms, and when he stopped running, he didn't have the strength to start again.

That's when he saw it.

A bright light illuminated through the trees. He heard a clashing sound, like a million construction workers hammering metal. It was followed by the roar of a billion growls and chuckles, one right after the other. The noise grew louder, and the blinding light never ceased to shine. Benji spun around, facing the familiar darkness once again, his eyes wide. Whatever was beyond those trees, he wasn't sure he was ready to know.

He felt the last of his oxygen sucked out of his body, as if some invisible being had punched him in the gut. Each breath was more rapid than the last. He tried to breathe steadily, but the air continued to slip. Falling right in front of him. Tangling itself in his shaking fingertips as his heart pounded faster. Faster and faster, beyond control.

Adrenaline rushed through him. His legs twitched from the inside, eager to rush into the woods and away from danger, but too exhausted. Crossing a threshold of panic, he leaned forward, preventing his insides from slipping out of his mouth. He was tumbled in a bag. Everything spun, and his area of vision grew smaller by the second.

The rain rushed mercilessly. It showered him in waterfalls, streaming from his fingertips into a puddle formed at his feet. It took all of his strength to face the shining lights a second time. He moved forward slowly, weighed by the heavy water that submersed his ankles.

The water started to move.

The pool rushed in circles, attempting to trip him. As the rain intensified, the water grew taller. It reached his knees.

Benji took another step, but the ground beneath him declined, leaving the water deeper than before. The raindrops summoned waves that stole Benji's control. He lost his grip on the dirt, pulled away from it by the frosty water. His legs scrambled, searching for support, but it wasn't there.

The water raised to his neck, and Benji slipped below the surface.

CHAPTER 35

gone

Drip. Drip. Plop.

The rain accumulated on the overhang of Ms. Camille's shop, dripping onto the concrete in hefty bulbs. Under the dense gray sky, James watched the water fall from the neon green shop and burst against the ground. Mist fell on Wishville, dampening his clothes, and he shivered. The date was May 30th, a week since Benji left, and it was a week where gloom filled the town more than ever.

James stood by the courtyard fountain, the light rain trickling down his windbreaker, the flow of water surrounding him—trickling through the fountain, plopping from the building overhangs, streaming down the side of Main Street. He flipped the hood over his head. The green paint was all he had left of Benji, and he found himself coming here without even knowing it.

The building was closed. Ms. Camille had decided to retire only a few days ago. Now the flower shop stood empty in the square, not a single bloom in sight through its new window.

"James!" A figure rushed toward him through the

courtyard. Lauren had one hand on her head, as if it might somehow protect her from the rain. She dropped it to set her arm around his shoulder, leading him into Seaside Cafe.

The building was warm. Lauren set him at the closest table and shot a look at Ricky, who nodded and brewed a new drink. James's icy hands stung as they thawed.

With the normally-filled tables of Seaside Cafe deserted, it seemed like Lauren and Ricky had nothing more to do than talk and stare at the rain.

"Hey, you can't keep doing this." Lauren sat across from him, and James faced the wooden table, observing its grain. "At some point, you're gonna have to go back to school."

Ricky spilled a pot of beans behind the counter, and Lauren frowned. "Keep it down over there!"

"Sorry, I just . . ." He took a deep breath before leaning over to clear the mess.

"You're a smart kid." Lauren grinned. "There's only a week until graduation, and you need to be there."

James grew sick at the thought of going to school. He wanted to stay in his room, curled comfortably under the covers, ridden with guilt. Lauren didn't understand that school was the least of his worries. How could it be more important to him than Benji?

Somehow, she read his mind. "This isn't about Benji anymore, it's about you. And by you, I mean all of you."

"All?"

"Think about Sam and Chloe." James shivered, and Lauren stood to wrap her scarf around his neck. "They need you as much as you need them."

He was warmer now, besides his feet. They were

numb, coated with a layer of wet socks. For the first time that James could remember, he wanted to cry. He wouldn't, of course, but the urge lingered. And as Ricky set a mug and blueberry muffin in front of him, James used every ounce of strength in his body to raise his head and thank him.

The two watched him eat. The muffin scratched its way down his throat, and each sip of coffee made him more nauseous than the one before. He didn't care that he wasn't a coffee drinker, or the fact that he hated sweets. He choked it all down faster than he could taste. How long had it been since he last ate?

"Your parents must be worried." Lauren leaned against the backrest and crossed her arms. "They know you came here, right?"

James nodded. "They—they know I need time."

The muffin vanished, and his mug emptied out. Ricky pulled it from him immediately. "I'll get more."

James waited for Ricky to reach the counter before speaking again. "I lost my sister, and now my best friend." His voice was raspy. "If I had just—"

"Stop." Lauren's stare burned him until he finally looked into her eyes. "Listen to me. Everyone feels guilty right now. You think I don't? The night before Benji left, I arranged for Sam to come talk to him. If I'd never done that, they wouldn't have made plans to meet. Maybe none of this would've happened. You think I never feel guilty about that?"

James yearned to look away from her, but no matter how much willpower he used, he couldn't manage it.

"Everyone feels what you're feeling, but are you just gonna watch them sulk? Or are you gonna stand up and tell them they're not alone?" Lauren shut her eyes for a moment, holding her composure. "Because right now, that's what I'm telling you."

James allowed her words into his mind, although he wasn't sure what any of it meant. Eventually, Ricky returned with another cup of coffee, and James gulped it down faster than the last.

The empty cafe was colorless, but chatting with Lauren had somehow brought a hint of color into the room. The air filled with a warm orange hue, lighting everything with a dewy glow. Maybe—just maybe—she was right. Perhaps he wasn't alone.

"Are you saying I should go to school?" James set his empty mug on the table.

She stared out the window, watching the seagulls gather in colonies by the sea. "I think that if Benji were here, he'd want you three together."

"You tried to kill him," Sam muttered.

Mayor Perkins had his hands wrapped loosely around the steering wheel. "Of course I didn't." He caught Sam's eyes for a moment, and she turned to the window, watching the trees whiz past them.

"You tried to shoot him." Sam hugged the backpack on her lap, pulling it into her chest. Her brothers sat in the back seat, silent. They hadn't been told a hint about the tragic night last week, although after Sam and the mayor's frequent arguments, they had probably pieced together the story by now.

"No, that's not what it was." He sighed. "For the hundredth time, I never intended to harm him. All I needed was a way to pressure him into the car. How else could I help? Samantha, he was willing to leave town—to leave everyone behind. The only threat strong enough to faze him was death before leaving. You know I did the right thing."

Sam banged a fist on the car door, her head boiling. "You did anything *but* the right thing, okay?" Her eyes watered. "This whole time, you never cared about Benji. You didn't even *try* to understand him!"

He raised his voice. "I did everything I could to keep him safe."

"You tried to kill him."

"He almost got in the car."

"You tried to kill him."

"If you hadn't interfered, I would've driven him home that night."

"You tried to kill him." Sam's backpack fell to the car floor, and she breathed into her palms. "I never should've told you about how he tried to leave. I shouldn't have held a grudge over some stupid argument. If only I'd gotten over it and—"

"Samantha." His voice was stern, and his grip intensified on the steering wheel. "You did the right thing by telling us."

Sam didn't know which was right—telling the adults about Benji's failed escape, or helping him leave last week. No matter how many times she told Mayor Perkins he did wrong, the guilt never left her. She couldn't help but wonder if it was her who tried to kill him. Maybe Mayor Perkins was right. Maybe if she stayed home that night—if she never agreed to meet at Blueberry—Benji would still be alive.

"I'm getting out here." She retrieved her backpack from the floor.

"If you want to make things harder on yourself," he pulled over to the side of the road and gestured to the door, "go right ahead."

"You're gonna be late," one of the twins said.

"Oh, shut up." Sam stormed out of the passenger seat and onto the sidewalk. As soon as she shut the door behind her, the car zoomed down the road without hesitation.

An arm wrapped around her shoulder. Tobias had abandoned the safety of the back seat to join her. They walked to school together in silence.

Sam had dreaded class lately. Everyone was shocked about Benji leaving town, but no one knew she was there when it happened. She intended to keep it that way, but it was painful to bottle the truth inside of her. Listening to their few pieces of the jigsaw puzzle made her sick.

She walked slowly, hoping to show up as late as possible. Instead of rushing, Tobias matched her pace.

"You'll be late," Sam said.

"I know."

"Your finals are coming up."

"So?"

"And now Dad's gonna be mad at you, too."

"Let him."

There was a certain spark in Tobias' eyes that she hadn't seen before, and she welcomed it.

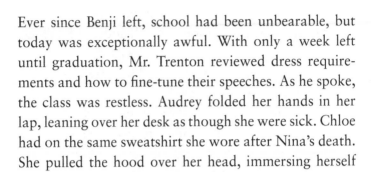

Ever since Benji left, school had been unbearable, but today was exceptionally awful. With only a week left until graduation, Mr. Trenton reviewed dress requirements and how to fine-tune their speeches. As he spoke, the class was restless. Audrey folded her hands in her lap, leaning over her desk as though she were sick. Chloe had on the same sweatshirt she wore after Nina's death. She pulled the hood over her head, immersing herself deeper into the darkness, and this time, Mr. Trenton didn't mind.

Chloe peeked at James's desk. Still empty. He hadn't come to school since he heard the news that night.

"I know you're all dealing with some..." Mr. Trenton paused. "*Things*. But it's important to focus right now. In only a week, you'll be out of here."

"Focus?" Jett held his back straight in his seat for once, feet firmly on the floor. "How do you expect us to focus with Benji dead?"

Dead.

The word hit Chloe like a bullet. It was an avoided word, always replaced with softer terms like *lost* or *gone* or *left*. No one but Jett was brave enough to say it, yet now that the word floated through the air, the students loosened.

"I know it's not easy." Mr. Trenton broke a grin. "But don't forget that your big day is coming up. Pretty soon, you'll be high schoolers, running around with the *big kids*."

"I don't care about school right now." Audrey leaned her head on her desk. "Can't we go home for the week?"

Peyton sniffled. "Can't we go home forever?"

"Or just skip graduation?" Noah added. "I'd rather not go."

"This is non-negotiable," Mr. Trenton said. "Graduation is your big day."

Chloe rubbed her eyes. "Well it was Benji's big day, too." And maybe if she hadn't turned against him at Blueberry, everything would be okay. Maybe if she trusted him and never vandalized Stricket's home, Benji would be sitting in class with her, breathing the same air.

Mr. Trenton broke his eyes from the room, focusing on his desk. He stacked a few piles of paperwork and sorted through them. Stamping them. Turning them. Filling them with more marks than necessary.

Sam rose from her seat, her sharp words penetrating the dense air. "I thought Benji was one of your favorite students."

Mr. Trenton stared at Sam with marbles for eyes. His grip tightened on the paper in his hands.

"I don't know what the heck happened that night," Jett said. "But you know what? I'm glad he stole my bike."

Noah removed his glasses and rubbed his eyes. "He knew how to ride a bike?"

Sam bit her lip as she sat, concealing a grin.

"Shocking, right?" Jett's smile was contagious. It spread through the room, and soon everyone was laughing. Even Chloe.

"Alright, that's enough." Mr. Trenton made eye

contact with each of them, killing the humor one student at a time.

But when his eyes met Chloe's, she sensed the same guilt that plagued her.

Rebecca hadn't been up Candy Road in years—ten years, to be exact. Shutting her eyes, she imagined her son walking down the same path. The thought made her nauseous. She wrapped two hands around her mouth, forcing herself to breathe through her nose in hopes that it'd get rid of that suffocating burn in her throat.

It didn't.

One foot in front of the other, she walked across the bridge. It felt so foreign to her. So dangerous. So thrilling. When she reached the center, she leaned over the railing, watching the town like a seagull from above. She couldn't deny the fact that it was a beautiful view. Wishville was a painting. It didn't look real.

Her hair spun in the wind like a delicate sheet waving from a clothespin. The breeze was fresh, with a dash of salt. She shut her eyes, listening to the waves below her, feeling the tears seep over her cheeks. "I wish I let you play soccer," she said. "I wish I didn't hide those photos. I wish I gave you more space." She shook her head.

"I wish I didn't consider you *his* son. I wish I thought of you as mine."

The waves drowned out thoughts, leaving her with a clear mind. She faced the *LEAVING WISHVILLE* sign, staring it in the eye, as her husband and son both had. She took a few steps toward the edge, peeking at the abyss through the trees. She could see nothing there. Just a dark path leading into a world many chose not to know. With a deep breath, she turned away from the sign and wrapped her cold fingers around the bridge railing.

She shut her eyes, clearing her mind of all thoughts. Her arms trembled in the chilling air, leaving her body numb, and her mind empty. Her head was a mass of indescribable colors, floating around as indescribable shapes. She let the colors soak her mind as she planted her right foot on the railing, opened her eyes, and took a final breath.

It was so bright.

So colorful.

So warm.

And she wished it could last forever.

CHAPTER 36

hartfield

Benji floated in a thick fluid. With numb nerves he tried to move, but could feel nothing. He couldn't tell whether his eyes were open or closed. Either way, he was positive the air must have been dyed black.

An oval of vision formed in front of him, the splattering of darkness inching away from his eyes until he could see. In that moment, all that existed was a room of white walls, and a blinding light fixture hanging above him. Gazing into the bulb, a warmth overcame him that later morphed into a burning sensation. His brain thawed, and his nerves slammed back into place. He realized he was lying on a stiff bed, his body covered with a single sheet.

The room was not only white, but close to empty. There was nothing but the bed, a fluffy pillow, a door on the right, and a window on the wall across from him. It was covered in thick, gray drapes, and Benji could sense the unimaginable hidden behind it. He sat and reached for his forehead, searching for some kind of memory.

"Please, calm down." A man appeared at his bedside with a clipboard in hand. He was dressed in casual clothes, yet a fancy plate sewn into the left side of his chest read *Dr. Bard*. Benji assumed he was around forty by the way his eyes held a strange depth.

"There's nothing to be afraid of. I only have a few questions." He lifted a pen to his notepad. "Will you give me your name and age, please?"

Benji. My name is Benji. A burning filled his lungs, and he coughed. *I'm 14.* The memories flooded him in overwhelming waves, one directly after the next. The ticking in his head was gone, and he missed it. "What time is it?" He remembered Wishville, and how he left. He remembered his time with James, Sam, and Chloe. He remembered the night of May 23rd, when the mayor pulled a gun on him at the bridge. When Sam nearly fell. Raising his empty wrist, he remembered how Oliver helped him. His watch was gone, but the memory wasn't. "What day is it? Where am I?" He ran his fingers through his hair, his brain failing him. "I don't get it. I drowned. I died!"

"Relax," the man reminded him. "I know you must have a lot of questions, but you need to trust that I'm here to help." He held out his hand. "I'm Dr. Bard. It's a pleasure to meet you."

Benji stared at the floating hand. "What's that?"

"My bad. I forget it's a cultural thing." He raised his arm a bit, repeating the gesture. "It's a hand shake. Something we do here when meeting someone new."

Benji blinked, and Dr. Bard pulled his hand away. "You'll get it eventually." He set his notepad on the edge of the bed. "Let's talk about what happened. Do you remember how you got here?"

"No, but I—I'm supposed to be dead." As Benji ran

his fingers along his bandaged right arm, he could nearly hear the shattering glass. "Last night. I was supposed to die. Why am I here? Why do—"

"Give me a moment, will you?" Dr. Bard stepped to the other side of the room, planting his feet firmly by the window. With one swift motion, he pulled the drapes away.

Through that window was a world Benji never could have dreamed of. Intricate structures as imaginary as the ones in his sketchbook. Buildings that reached the clouds. Streets crowded with too many faces to count. The view merged into a single blob of energy.

But most importantly, he saw colors.

Brilliant colors. Some radiated out of windows, and others tinted the clouds in batches. He saw colors he couldn't name. Colors he didn't know existed.

The rising sun shined brighter than he'd ever seen in Wishville. Its rays trickled over the roofs of structures and onto the glimmering roads and walkways below. The already-radiant colors sparkled indefinitely. No ocean. No trees. Just colors. Light.

Benji gulped. "Where are we?"

"Where do you think we are?"

"I don't—I—"

"Welcome to Hartfield." Dr. Bard set a hand on his chest.

Benji couldn't take his eyes off the window.

"See all those people out there? They left their old lives for a better one. Abandoned their homes. Their families. All for the unknown." He leaned against the wall. "I came from a place called Living Heights. I hated my life there, so I thought I might as well leave it behind.

And here I am." He lost his eyes in the distance. "Us ex-Heighters joke about it sometimes. It's funny how it's called *Living* Heights when we felt dead being there." He paused, waiting for Benji to speak, but the room sat in silence. He pulled the drapes shut. "Any other questions for me?"

"Hartfield?" He shook his head. "So you're telling me everyone who left ended up *here*?"

"Precisely."

"But why wouldn't they come back and tell us? Wouldn't they want to let us know? What's the point in leaving it a mystery?"

"Jeez, you sure do ask a lot of questions." The man chuckled. "Once you're in Hartfield, you can consider your old life dead."

"Dead . . ." Benji frowned. "But what if—"

"I think I explained enough for now." He swiped his notepad from the edge of the bed. "You'll understand with time. Now can you give me your name and age, please?"

"Benji Marino. I'm fourteen."

Dr. Bard scribbled on his notepad. "And where are you from?"

"Wishville."

His pen paused over the paper. "Been a while since I last heard of that one." The man tapped his fingers against the clipboard as he headed to the door. "I'll be right back."

Dr. Bard disappeared into the hall before Benji could ask any more questions. He slid out of bed, his feet landing on a pair of sneakers with socks wadded inside them. They were new. That's when he realized he was no longer wearing what he wore on the 23rd. He had a pair of blue jeans on, topped with a simple white t-shirt.

As Benji slipped the socks on, a mumbling echoed in the hall. Escalating to a shout, the door slammed open, and Dr. Bard walked in, followed by another unfamiliar face.

The boy didn't look too much older than Benji. He was around James's height, but his skin was so pale that Benji could see the veins running through his crossed arms. His blond hair flopped over the side of his head, forming a heavy pile of bangs. He narrowed his eyes at Benji, flinching as Dr. Bard swung an arm over his shoulder.

"Thought I was done with guide duty," he muttered.

Benji put the shoes on. They fit perfectly.

"Meet Porter," Dr. Bard said. "He'll be showing you around."

Benji held his arm out in front of him. "Nice to meet you."

Porter didn't move. "I'm standing ten feet away."

"Is that bad?"

"Let's skip the handshake." Porter turned and opened the door to a hallway of blinding light. "Follow me."

Benji could see.

A layer of his eyes had peeled away, leaving his sight rich and vulnerable. Everywhere he turned he could see. He could see too much. Smell too much. Hear too much. It was all new. All fresh. All paralyzing.

They stood outside the entrance to the hospital building, the end of a long concrete pathway lined with cherry blossoms. People walked by, dressed in the most ridiculous clothing. They spoke in tongues he couldn't understand. Walked in a rhythmic pattern he couldn't decipher. Their eyes were glazed over, bored, although vivid. This world was a new reality for them.

Buildings blocked the sun in every direction, but the light never faded. Giant boards on the sides of buildings flashed with brilliant colors. Adults in suits chatted with coffee cups in hand. Most of the people in town were elderly, some adults, and the rare child. A boy around the age of seven ran down the pathway, pivoted around Benji, and continued down the side road. He was playing tag, running from another boy slightly older than him. The older one stopped and made eye contact with Benji. He smiled.

Benji couldn't smile back.

"It's a lot to take in." Porter chuckled to himself.

Faces everywhere. Faces he couldn't recognize. How could so many people exist?

"Let's walk. You'll see less that way."

Benji followed him in a trance.

"Your arm," Porter said after a moment of silence. "How'd it happen?"

Benji squinted at the bandage. It took a moment to recall. "I broke a window."

"How?" He struck a fist through the air in front of him. "You punched it?"

"Not exactly."

"Oh?" Porter grinned. "Fun."

They walked for a while. The pathway led deeper

through Hartfield. The further they walked, the fewer people crossed their path. It grew silent. Birds flapped between trees. Foreign birds of exotic colors. No seagulls. The pests he grew up hating, despising, envying. They were no more.

"Where are you taking me?" Benji asked.

Porter pursed his lips, and Benji didn't question him further. They walked until the sun had fully risen, filling the sky with new shades of colors and unique fluffs of clouds. Through a clump of buildings a few feet away, he saw something familiar.

Evergreen.

Redwoods.

Tall, slender trees.

Porter stopped, and Benji faced the stretch of the walkway behind them. In one glance, he filled his mind with an image that would take hours to process. There was so much. Too much.

He ran.

Benji ran off the concrete walkway. He ran toward the trees. The world where he lived to leave and now could not live with leaving. His shoes burned against the hot pavement. Cars came to a sudden stop. No one tried to stand in his way. Instead, they watched him with familiar eyes.

"Benji!" He could hear Porter's raspy voice behind him. "Don't go there! Not yet."

It was too late. Benji sprinted between two massive redwood trees. He felt the dirt under his shoes. The sour smell of forest. Everything was familiar.

He recognized a road and slowed down. It had to be the same path. The dirt around him was moist, some areas containing miniature puddles. With the sun out, the path was much clearer. Almost beautiful. He walked the forbidden woods not once, but twice.

I have to tell them. Benji ran again. He ran so fast that it felt as though the ground might slip from under him. So fast that he might shoot into the sky and float with the stars. So fast that his thoughts nearly ceased to exist. He didn't know anything. Not how to think. How to feel. All he knew was *run.*

He followed the curve in the road. Trickles of blue ocean appeared between the trees. This was the end.

He walked.

Pump. Pump. His heart beat heavily as he slowed his pace, approaching the end of the road. A few more steps and he'd run into the bridge. He'd find them. He'd share the truth with them.

He'd save them.

A cliff.

At the end of the road, there was no bridge. No island waiting for him.

No Wishville.

"You weren't supposed to see this yet." Porter appeared beside him, watching the waves thrash at the bottom of the cliff.

A vast ocean. That was it. Benji couldn't form words. What could he say?

"I know how you feel. We've all been in your shoes." Porter stepped away from the ledge. "But it's time to move on. There's no going back."

Benji's eyes traced the horizon. Nothing.

"They'll come when they're ready." There was a

softness to his voice. It was welcoming, and Benji had a strange desire to turn his back to the ocean.

"Porter?" Benji's arms stiffened. "Where am I?"

CHAPTER 37

graduation

June 6th arrived faster than Chloe dreaded.

The gym was decorated with three years' worth of science projects, art, and awards, none of which were Benji's. All of Wishville shared an unspoken understanding that the boy's name was forbidden. Not to be spoken, not to be written, and certainly not to be displayed.

After progressing down the aisle, the eighth-grade class sat in the front row. The music faded, and Mr. Trenton appeared on stage. He was dressed in a suit, a raspy microphone in hand.

"Thank you for joining us in celebrating this year's graduating class . . ."

While he babbled over his enjoyment of teaching, Chloe studied the fabric of her red dress. She had tried to enjoy shopping for it, but by the time she left the store, her sister was practically forcing it into her arms.

The day was finally here.

"I admire every one of your students. They are all *so* unique, and have *so* much potential. I couldn't be prouder." Mr. Trenton cleared his throat, sending a buzzing noise through the room. Parents shrieked, and the front row of gloomy students broke a grin, although only for a moment. "Looks like even the microphone is excited." The crowd forced a laugh, and he waited for the room to settle before continuing.

"This year has not been easy for anyone, but we've made it through together." His students' remaining smiles permanently chipped away. "It is an honor to have been their eighth-grade homeroom teacher." A pause. "And now, it is time for our students to present their speeches." He set the microphone on the podium with a click, and backed away to a roar of applause. Chloe didn't clap.

We've made it through together. She huffed at the words.

The more people who presented behind that podium, the more uncomfortable Chloe became, and that wasn't because it was almost her turn. Many kids had grown teary-eyed during the strangest parts, like mentions about the science they learned, or how valuable the school library was for research. Chloe cringed at the awed parents. She knew the real reason behind their emotion had nothing to do with academics, and with the thought came tears. She held them back with a gulp.

It was her turn to speak.

As Chloe walked up the steps, she wished the night could be over. She pictured herself ripping off the uncomfortable dress, chugging a gallon of ice cream, and slipping into bed for the rest of summer.

She stood at the podium now, the rows of chairs uncountable, each face small and insignificant. She grabbed the microphone and flipped the binder page to reveal her speech reference—the outline they were required to craft as a guide. She scanned over the first section with a frown.

"At the beginning of this year," she said, "I was shyer than I am now. I struggled with speaking in front of adults, but with the help of Mr. Trenton, I've had the chance to overcome these obstacles. I've grown not only academically, but socially. This final year has more than prepared me for my future education, and I couldn't be more grateful for Wishville Junior High."

She paused for a breath, using the moment to observe the crowd's reactions. In the third row, Audrey's mom sat wiping her damp cheek, still moved from the previous speech. Chloe's free hand rolled into a fist, hidden behind the podium. The speeches were exactly what everyone wanted to hear—crafted with the image of pleasing the students' families, teachers, and staff.

But they were lies.

She realized that she'd been silent for an awkward amount of time. Sam shuffled in her seat. Everyone had sat through each other's speeches multiple times during practices, and Chloe had never taken such long pauses before.

She scanned her speech outline a final time before disregarding it.

"During this past year, I've lost more than I ever imagined."

Her classmates raised their chins in unison, the gloom forming a unity between them. The truth was painful, yet something about it was oddly comforting.

"I didn't only lose a best friend. I lost everything. My love for softball. My excitement for school. My interest in science was replaced with an interest in blame." She loosened her fist. "We've been expected to pretend like nothing changed. Like we didn't lose one of the most cheerful students in town. But things *have* changed. Benji's gone. My best friend is gone."

The room shifted, spectators positioning themselves in their seats as if the environment might reverse to how it used to be. Mr. Trenton stared at Chloe with bird eyes, and Coach Hendrick lifted his stiff back off the wall, facing the front of the room with his mustache forming a line.

"This year was the worst year of my life."

She raced down the stairs on the opposite end of the stage, the microphone slipping from her hand.

"Chloe!" Mr. Trenton stepped in her direction as the microphone tumbled off the stage and landed with a violent squeal. She paused, looking over her shoulder to see the crowd erupting in shouts, hands over their ears.

Panic rushing through her veins, she disappeared through the back door.

The thought of a student running to an unknown destination was perhaps the new worst nightmare of Wishville. Panic flooded the gym. Parents muttered foul words and pulled young children close to them. When the screeching diminished, James stood from his seat, Lauren's voice filling his mind.

"Everyone feels what you're feeling, but are you just gonna watch them sulk? Or are you gonna stand up and tell them they're not alone?"

His heart pounded all the way to his head. Not bothering to question his emotions, he stepped toward the door. "I'll find her."

The rowdy room fell still at the rare sound of James's voice.

"I'm coming with you."

A hint of charcoal fabric taunted his focus. He knew Sam was next to him, but refrained from making eye contact. Instead, he watched her flats smack against the gym floor. It was the first time he'd seen her without her rustic sneakers in years.

"Hey!" Mayor Perkins' voice boomed through the room, paralyzing James and Sam. "No one's leaving this room. *I'll* bring her back."

"But what about the service?" Mrs. Zhao tucked a strand of ashy hair behind her ear. "We can't cancel graduation for one spoiled girl."

Audrey's face broke into disgust. "Mom!"

Mr. Koi adjusted his glasses. "Arthur will find her quickly."

"And if he doesn't?" Mrs. Zhao crossed her arms. "We stand here waiting to hear news of another child runaway?"

Mr. Koi's face did not budge. "Let's calm down."

"*You* calm down!"

The fuzzy atmosphere escalated into a rugged home of disoriented parents, confused siblings, and a string of classmates living in the past. Benji was gone. He not only left town, but he also left the chaos behind him. His stress of leaving, the wretched curiosity, and the strenuous guilt washed over him and into Wishville through a storm. Benji's action had yet to be defined. A crime? A sacrifice? A mistake? What exactly did leaving mean, and what should it mean to them? What should they fear? What should they hope for?

James heard the questions, too. They throbbed in his brain, leaving his head sore and muscles tense. Attempting to regain cognitive balance, he counted. *One, two, three . . .*

"That's enough!" Mayor Perkins' voice boomed through the room, silencing the burning thoughts that filled them.

James's muscles relaxed. By the time he reached the present, Mayor Perkins' had retrieved the microphone from the floor. "I understand that our students are in a bit of a fritz right now, but I'd like to ask you to stay calm so we can work our way through this."

James nodded at Sam, and she reached for the door.

"Samantha!"

Before her fingers touched the knob, she dropped her wrist. "Go without me," she whispered. Mayor Perkins had every intent to keep her here.

James bit his lip. They'd have no chance to talk until the adults gave them time, and they both knew it. He narrowed his eyes, searching for something extravagant to do. Something convincing to say.

He flinched as a figure hopped onto the stage with a spirited leap.

Jett towered over the crowd, filled with energy. The sight of him standing so confidently eased the tension in the air. He raised his voice to ensure that every soul in the gym could hear him. "If there's one thing I've learned this year," he said, "it's that sometimes, it's okay to run away." His voice echoed through the gym, and the room grew to a new level of silence.

Mr. Trenton leaned against the wall, and Coach Hendrick raised his chin with a chuckle.

Mayor Perkins' brows formed a curvy road on his head, his arms crossed so tight that his fingers went pale. It was the first time James had heard Sam speak to the man softly. "Please?"

The mayor's body relaxed. With his eyebrows curved normally again, his arms relaxed, and fingers breathing, he gave a slight nod. Almost a non-existent one, but to the two of them, it was prominent. He tossed the microphone up the stage, and Jett swiped it from the air.

"I never really got along with Benji. I know he was never one of my fans." Jett shrugged. "But even I feel guilty. I can't even imagine how hard it is on people he was actually friends with, you know?" He took a deep breath and raised his voice one final time. "So parents, I'm asking that you give these three losers a chance to talk."

At first it was only one. Just one smile from a man in the back row. But soon that smile spread into a massive, collective grin. The gym lights radiated a dull warmth, and saturation struck the room. The blue and green banners jumped off the walls into the air, and as people inhaled the colors, James noticed their vibrant clothing for the first time. A boy in the front row wore a collared shirt the shade of a tangerine with thin, creamy stripes running vertically across it. In the far end of the row, a lady unzipped her furry pink jacket, revealing a shimmering silver top. Even Sam's dress—although charcoal gray—had a hint of blue to it, as though she wore the midnight sea.

Mayor Perkins and his navy blazer collided with the ocean of color. The smiles morphed into claps, and claps into cheers. Some adults grew teary-eyed, and although the younger siblings could not comprehend the magnitude of such a strange graduation, they laughed at the thought that someday, they'd graduate eighth grade, too.

Standing on the stage under a golden spotlight, Jett saluted James in a playful wish of good luck.

A silhouette wavered behind a thick layer of trees. Sam rushed between branches, watching the waves dance, calling her. Twigs crunched under her feet, and bushes scraped at her bare legs, but she pushed forward, the pounding of James's footsteps echoing behind her.

The figure was clearly Chloe now. Her brown hair waved in the air, blown by the buttery wind. Sam ran faster, and once she reached the sand, kicked her shoes off and rushed to the shore.

Chloe sat at the delicate point where dry met damp, facing the waves. Sam and James joined her on opposite sides—not close enough for it to be obvious the three were together, but close enough to question if they were strangers. They lost their thoughts in the horizon, and at that moment, the ocean was all that mattered.

"I wish Benji was here today." Chloe drew cute little shapes in the sand with her index finger.

Sam's eyes swayed with the water's flow. "We all do."

The waves rippled, and the pressure between them chipped away.

"I—I think there's something you guys should know," Chloe said.

Sam wanted to look in Chloe's direction, but she locked her neck, not wanting to pressure her. James did the same.

Chloe scooped a batch of sand into her hand, feeling it seep between his fingers. "I was the one who vandalized Oliver's house."

The beach was quiet. Sam bit her lip, and the smell of salt filled her lungs. She had nothing to say to Chloe. Part of her wanted to be angry. To lash out of her, but that anger didn't seem to exist. All that lingered was guilt. Chloe wasn't the only one who had regrets.

"Guess it's my turn, then." Sam threw her legs out in front of her, letting the heels of her feet rest in the soft side of the sand. "I was mad at Benji, so I spilled his secret about how he tried to leave. And at the worst time, too. I was a real idiot. Had a million chances to apologize, but I never did."

In that moment, it didn't matter why Benji left. It didn't matter whose fault it was. The important fact was that they knew the truth. That they had *shared* the truth.

"I miss my sister."

Sam and Chloe looked over at James, who quickly wiped his eyes with the sleeve of his blazer.

Chloe set an arm on his shoulder. "We know."

"When she died, everything changed, and I was confused." He spoke with a tremble in his voice. A certain vibration of regret they had never heard in him before.

"I have a confession, too. The reason Mayor Perkins found you at Blueberry was because I told him about your plan. Maybe if I trusted you instead of staying home, everything would be different."

"I'm sorry," Sam said. "To Benji, and to both of you, too."

"Me too," Chloe said.

James nodded. "Sorry."

The murky sun set slowly, but as its glow skimmed the horizon, the sky lit with an explosion of water. Red branches reached out from the sun, spreading into the sky with an orange glow. The gray ocean intensified to a striking blue. Wisps of pink rained from the sky into the water, bursting into pops of blinding light that raced back and forth across the surface, never submersing themselves. The three hadn't realized it, but they'd scooted closer to each other. Close enough to be obvious they were together. Close enough to be obvious they were friends.

Chloe's eyes radiated the melting colors. "I've never seen anything like it."

"You think there's more out there?" Sam pointed at the ocean. "Past that weird line in the sky?"

"I don't know." James bit his lip.

Sam leaned back, supporting herself with her arms. "Do you think Benji did the right thing?" The colors soaked into her, accompanied by a warmth that inched through her skin. Her hair stopped blowing in her face, the wind reaching a halt. It was almost like the clock had stopped ticking. Time had slowed to a point where she could no longer feel it.

"I don't know what's right anymore." Chloe patted

the sand next to her, the drawings she'd made vanishing forever.

"Me neither." James shrugged. "And I don't think it's for us to decide."

The sun lowered, slowly slipping from their sight. The brilliant colors in the sky lost a hint of vividness, and Sam clung to the remaining hues with her life.

"You've got the worst luck." Chloe jabbed Sam in the side. "Your first crush literally disappears."

Sam rolled her eyes. "Not funny."

"So you don't deny it."

"Is this really the best time to joke around?"

"Finally." Chloe gave James a high five. "She didn't deny it!" The two of them smiled.

Sam crossed her arms with a huff. "Wait till Jett finds out the culprit was right in front of his nose this whole time."

"You wouldn't dare!" Chloe shook her head until the redness in her cheeks disappeared.

"Stop." James threw a clump of sand into the ocean. "Let's not argue."

Sam rolled her eyes. "As if *you're* any more innocent."

"Yeah, if it weren't for you then maybe . . ." Chloe frowned. "What's so funny?"

James leaned over his stomach, shaking. It started as a gentle laugh, his hysteria slowly escalating until his face was beet red. His laughing morphed into what sounded like a violent attack of hiccups. Chloe and Sam met eyes and joined with hysteria. Three from a set of four, laughing together at the ocean, the wind twisting their hair as the colors faded from the sky.

With the sun nearly gone, they stood and gave each

other hugs. The word *congratulations* echoed between them.

They didn't graduate with a handshake from Mr. Trenton. They didn't graduate the moment they said the last word of their speeches on stage. Even with their first step from the gym that summer day, they had yet to graduate. Their real graduation was here, on the sand. It was the moment they were truly ready to move on. And as they prepared to leave the ocean behind and head back inside, Sam found herself restraining tears.

"Hey." Chloe nudged her arm. "You okay?"

"You guys go on ahead." Sam stepped toward the shore. "I'm gonna stay a bit longer."

"You just don't wanna thank Jett for once." Chloe grinned as she slipped her shiny flats back on.

Sam chuckled. "*Sure.*"

"Don't deny it." James gave her head a quick shove. "I'm not looking forward to it either." With a warm smile, he was the first to leave down the path they had come from. Chloe waved Sam goodbye and trailed after him.

Sam stood alone on the sand, longing for the radiant glow that once drowned her vision. The colors had completely disappeared from the sky, and now that she had a taste of them, she wanted them back. Approaching the shoreline, she thought about Benji's first attempt to leave town, the night he finally did, and every moment in-between. The seagulls flapped their wings above her head, the world spinning beneath her feet.

"Benji Marino," she said with a grin. "What if you're right?"

With a final step, her feet sunk into the icy waves.

ACKNOWLEDGMENTS

I wrote the first draft of this novel as a high school freshman. After two years of time and dedication, Benji's story now sits in your hands, but I couldn't have done it alone.

First, I'd like to thank my amazing beta readers: Victoria Rose, Millie Florence, Serena Goshgarian, Marco Morano, Kathryn Dudley, Schuyler Jones, Meagan Lashinski, Amina Mehmood, Lucas James, Michael Evans, Abigail Ann, Hannah Xu, Dave Oliver, and Thomas Bottorff. Their honest critiques of my work pushed me in the right direction, and for that guidance I'm extremely grateful.

Big thanks to Ivan Cakamura, for his talented cover design, and my proofreaders—Janet Clark and James Hensley—for ensuring the novel reached its polished form.

Of course, I can't forget about my family. Mom, for imagining success with me. Dad, for helping me navigate the publishing challenges. John, for listening to my writing rants when I hit another dead end. While I'm at it, shoutout to Monica, Marie, Lucas, Levi, and Eli.

In the past few years I've connected with talented creatives through online communities. I'd like to thank the